# MEETING

# Books by
# NINA KIRIKI HOFFMAN

NINA KIRIKI HOFFMAN

# MEETING

## MAGIC NEXT DOOR BOOK II

WITHDRAWN

VIKING
An imprint of Penguin Group (USA) Inc.

VIKING
Published by Penguin Group
Penguin Young Readers Group, 345 Hudson Street, New York, New York 10014, U.S.A.
Penguin Group (Canada), 90 Eglinton Avenue East, Suite 700, Toronto, Ontario, Canada M4P 2Y3
(a division of Pearson Penguin Canada Inc.)
Penguin Books Ltd, 80 Strand, London WC2R 0RL, England
Penguin Ireland, 25 St Stephen's Green, Dublin 2, Ireland (a division of Penguin Books Ltd)
Penguin Group (Australia), 250 Camberwell Road, Camberwell, Victoria 3124, Australia
(a division of Pearson Australia Group Pty Ltd)
Penguin Books India Pvt Ltd, 11 Community Centre, Panchsheel Park, New Delhi – 110 017, India
Penguin Group (NZ), 67 Apollo Drive, Rosedale, Auckland 0632, New Zealand
(a division of Pearson New Zealand Ltd)
Penguin Books (South Africa) (Pty) Ltd, 24 Sturdee Avenue, Rosebank, Johannesburg 2196, South Africa

Penguin Books Ltd, Registered Offices: 80 Strand, London WC2R 0RL, England

First published in the U.S.A. by Viking, a member of Penguin Young Readers Group, 2011

1   3   5   7   9   10   8   6   4   2

LIBRARY OF CONGRESS CATALOGING-IN-PUBLICATION DATA
Hoffman, Nina Kiriki.
Meetings / Nina Kiriki Hoffman.
p. cm. — (Magic next door ; bk. 2)
Summary: Middle school student Maya Andersen and her family move to
Oregon, where the residents of the apartment building next to them have
magical powers and the basement is a portal to other worlds, which Maya
and her secret alien companion, Rimi, must use to track down aliens who
snatched Rimi from her home planet in an attempt to rule the universe.
ISBN 978-0-670-01283-1
[1. Magic—Fiction. 2. Kidnapping—Fiction. 3. Extraterrestrial beings—Fiction.]I. Title.
PZ7.H67567Me 2011
[Fic]—dc22
2011003002

Printed in U.S.A.
Set in Minion

To Devon Monk and Eric Witchey, co-conspirators
and late night e-mail buddies.

To Ashton (again) and Connor and Zack H.

To Sharyn, who works so hard with me
to make these books better.

Thank you all.

# MEETING

# ☀ ONE ☀

Maya Andersen held the front door wide on a crisp autumn Saturday night to let the neighbors into the Andersens' new house.

There were a lot of neighbors. She didn't know all of their names, even after having them over every Saturday Music Night for six weeks, and spending three days a week after school studying magic and related arts and sciences at Janus House, the big apartment building next door, where all these people lived. Every Music Night she tried to focus on new people, get their faces into her mind so she could draw them later and put names to them. Different people kept showing up, though. Where did they all come from?

Maybe the warren underneath Janus House, where the portal to other worlds was.

"Hi," she said as the people flowed inside, and most said, "Hello, Maya," as they passed her, or "Nice night!"

Five orange pumpkins perched on the porch railing. They glowed in the soft light spilling from the front windows and the open door. Maya's family had visited the pumpkin patch that afternoon. Halloween was a week away.

The air carried the spice of dead leaves, fallen, raked, stacked, jumped in. There was the tang of cold working on water. Smoke from the chimney flavored the air. Maya sniffed the mix of autumn scents, remembering last year, back in Idaho, when her best friend, Stephanie, had still been alive. Maya and Stephanie had been plotting their costumes for a week already by this time. Stephanie always dressed as something magical—a witch, a wizard, an elf, or, the year when they were six, a unicorn. Maya liked dressing as Steph's sidekick. If Steph was a witch, Maya dressed as a black cat to be her familiar. If Steph was a wizard, Maya might be a fellow wizard. Some years Steph dressed as something that didn't need a sidekick, like a fairy, and Maya went trick-or-treating as a Viking, in honor of the Andersen family heritage. She had a nice metal helmet with horns and rivets, and not enough occasions when she could wear it.

Steph had already started chemo by October of last year, and she'd lost her hair. She found a Lady Godiva wig at a Halloween store, blonde, curly hair that touched the ground. She dressed as Rapunzel, only Steph's Rapunzel had a magic wand with a crystal on the end. "It's the spirit of television," she had said, touching the crystal. "The witch can lock me in a tower, but I'll still find something to entertain me."

Maya had dressed as a ghost. She didn't want to do that again—not with Steph dead and not haunting, the way Maya and Steph had planned sometimes when they sat together in the middle of the night with the lights out near the end of Steph's life.

Maya wasn't sure who to be this year. She was living in a new house, in a new neighborhood, with lots of strange new friends, including one she wore like a shadow, Rimi.

Did Janus House people even celebrate Halloween?

Some of the neighbors carried plates covered with colorful dish towels. Some carried instrument cases. Some carried their own chairs. When the visitors ran out of room in the living room, where the piano was, they placed their chairs in the dining room and on the porch and settled. Those with food took the plates to the dining room table and set them down. Those with instrument cases opened the cases, got out instruments, and tuned.

Twelve-year-old Benjamin Porta crossed the porch, following two adults Maya didn't know yet. "Hey, Maya. Did you save me a seat?" He was just her height, with cinnamon skin, dark hair, and warm brown eyes with gold flecks in them. He wore a charcoal hoodie, blue jeans, and black tennis shoes.

"I put my coat over part of the couch," Maya said, pointing toward the couch near the piano. "Don't know if that worked." She peered past people to the couch. Nobody had sat on her coat yet, but two other people had claimed spots on the couch. There was still a space just wide enough for two, if they were small. "Guess it kinda did."

"Did you save *me* a seat?" asked Maya's other new friend from Janus House, Gwenda Janus. Gwenda was tall, pale, dark-haired, and slender, with eyes the color of sky. Tonight she was wearing a dark, full-length skirt with no stiffening to make it stand out. Her blouse was fairly subdued, for her: pale green with lines of white embroidery that showed vines and flowers.

Maya sighed. She had left her coat on enough of the couch to reserve space for three, but that hadn't worked.

"Just kidding," said Gwenda. "I brought my own chair." She held up a three-legged folded stool.

Maya kicked the doorstop under the doorsill—the door would have to stay open, anyway, so the people on the porch could hear—and the three of them made their way through the crowd to the couch.

The ancient witch and weaver Sarutha Gates, Maya's main Janus House teacher, was one of the people already sitting on the couch. Beside her was her almost-twin sister, Noona. Both of them had long silver-gray hair and wore dark velvet dresses.

Maya picked up her coat and put it on. The sisters smiled at Maya and Benjamin as they squeezed onto the couch, Maya between Benjamin and Sarutha. Gwenda set her stool nearby.

Maya's jean-clad leg pressed against Benjamin's jean-clad leg, and her shoulder was against his. He felt warm through all those layers, and he smelled like fresh bread and spices. She liked being next to him.

Maya's mother stood beside the piano, smiling at the company. She was short, pleasantly plump, and dark-haired, and she wore a light jacket over her clothes. Since fall had fallen, the nights were cool, but they had to keep all the windows open. When it froze, they might have to rethink the set-up. Dad had built up a fire in the fireplace, but the heat only went so far. People bundled up. "Welcome back, everyone," Mom said. "What's your pleasure tonight?"

Benjamin's mother, Dr. Porta, said, from the far side of the room, "Can we start off with 'Pretty Polly'?"

"Sure," said Mom. "What key?"

"A."

"And you want to do Polly's lines, right?"

Dr. Porta just smiled.

Mom sat at the piano. People with instruments put them into playable positions, and they all started the song on a downbeat from Maya's tall, blond father, who leaned against the wall near the piano.

Everybody sang about the evil Willy, who stabbed his girlfriend Pretty Polly through the heart, and her heart's blood did flow. Dr. Porta sang Pretty Polly's lines alone. "Willy, oh Willy, I'm afraid of your ways," Polly cried, as well she should be, since Willy's idea of a fun tour was to lead pretty Polly over the mountains and valleys to a grave he'd spent the night digging. Fear didn't save Pretty Polly, and begging didn't either. Willy stabbed her, threw her in the grave, and dropped a little dirt on her.

The Janus House people could harmonize like nobody's business. Maya wasn't sure whether to sing or listen. Maya's alien shadow, Rimi, was alive with delight; Maya felt her dancing, slight changes in air currents against Maya's face, and her joy was like warm water.

In the shuffle of the song's ending, Maya whispered to Benjamin, "Your mother."

He smiled. "My mother," he whispered.

*I like his mother*, Rimi thought.

*Me, too*, Maya thought.

Peter, Maya's younger brother, asked if they could sing "The Fox" next. Everybody got to pick at least one song on Music Night, which led to some very long nights. Janus House people seemed to know most of the folk songs the Andersens knew, and the ones they didn't know they learned after hearing them once or twice. The Andersens were still trying to learn Janus House people's favorite songs. The ones in English, anyway.

Sometimes the visitors sang songs in their own language, Kerlinqua, and then strange things happened. Winds blew only in the house. Little lights appeared in shadowed nooks and in spirals on the ceiling. Maya sometimes felt the brush of invisible wings, and sometimes she heard the whispers of people from otherwhere or otherwhen.

Sometimes the songs just made you feel different. Longing, sadness, or inexplicable happiness. Other songs could do that too, though.

Mom and Dad didn't seem to notice the magic sneaking in. Maya wondered if Peter did. He usually sat across the room from her on Music Night. Their seventeen-year-old sister Candra was off at her high school working on the school newspaper most Saturday nights. She had started resenting Music Night even before the family had moved from Idaho to Oregon.

"Let's never get that old," Maya and Peter had whispered to each other once, after Candra stomped off before the singing began.

Maya had always thought singing was magic. Her family used to have Music Night in Idaho and she loved the way songs could knit people together.

Candra was stupid to miss Music Night, Maya thought, as they went on to sing "The Springhill Mine Disaster." Candra was interested in journalism, and wildly curious about everything that happened next door, always trying to get Maya to talk about what she was learning, or what she saw and heard while she visited Janus House. Maya couldn't tell Candra anything. Silence lay on her tongue, put there by the leader of the Janus House people, Great-uncle Harper Janus.

If only Candra were here, she might notice strange things. Maybe she'd bug somebody besides Maya about it.

Halfway through the evening, when they broke for refreshments, Maya's wish came true. She had just loaded a plate with pumpkin bread from Benjamin's mother's kitchen when Candra came in the front door. Her pale hair haloed her head. Her black and gray school messenger bag hung against her hip. She stood on the threshold and looked at all the neighbors. Her green eyes lit. "Hey," she said. "Hey, y'all."

"You must be Candra. I'm Dr. Porta," said Benjamin's mother, from the chair closest to the door. "Would you like some cake?"

"Sure," said Candra. She shrugged out of her pack and followed Dr. Porta to the dining room table, glancing right and left as she went. People were sitting on chairs, with plates of food perched on their knees. Dr. Porta introduced Candra to other people, including Great-uncle Harper, not Maya's favorite person. Tonight Great-uncle Harper was wearing an orange suit. It looked like a business suit except for the color. Candra shook his hand enthusiastically, which Maya thought was a little careless; Harper was who knew how old, and he looked frail, like a good grip might break his bones. Deceptive, but how could Candra know that?

Maya took her plate and headed for the couch, wondering what had happened to Candra's newspaper night. She sat down and watched her sister charming strangers. Candra had the gift of being able to make people like her. Often they answered questions she asked when it would be much smarter if they didn't.

Gwenda settled next to Maya on the couch. She was watching Candra, too. "She lurks. She looms," she said. "I see her around Janus House all the time, despite the wards."

"She wants to find out all about you," Maya said.

"Oh, dear," said Gwenda.

"She can be incredibly snoopy and pesky."

"Oh, dear." Gwenda fingered the round, engraved stones of her charm bracelet.

*She strokes the power in them*, Rimi thought. *Different colors.*

*Can you show me?* Maya wondered.

*Hmm,* thought Rimi. A shadow dropped over Maya's eyes, and then something shifted in her vision and she saw that each of the stones on Gwenda's bracelet looked like a little galaxy, some red, some green, some gold, some blue. Gwenda's nervous fingers shifting them around made the galaxy lights flare or spread or collapse.

*Wow,* Maya thought. She blinked, and the shadow with its power of seeing energy flicked up and away. *Thanks, Rimi.* They were still getting to know each other. Every day brought more discoveries.

Candra made her way over and sat down on the couch next to Maya. "Hi, Gwenda. Nice to see you again," Candra said.

Gwenda had been Maya's first visitor in the new house; she had come to dinner soon after the Andersens moved in.

"Hi, Candra," Gwenda said.

"Last time I met you, I didn't know how interesting you were."

"I'm not interesting."

"Hey, I've seen how you dress. You're interesting."

"Thanks. I guess."

"I'd like to get a look in your closet," said Candra.

Gwenda turned and met Maya's eyes. No question,

Candra was snoopy. They smiled at each other.

"You are so subtle," Maya told her older sister.

Candra grinned and shrugged. "Come on, what's so secret about your closet?"

Gwenda cocked her head. Maya noticed that Gwenda's mean cousin Rowan had drifted closer, and so had Maya's Janus House teacher Sarutha.

"Well, maybe it'd be all right to show you," Gwenda said. She glanced at Sarutha, who nodded once. "How interested in clothes are you?"

"I like looking at people who wear a lot of colors. I don't necessarily want to wear them myself. When can I come?"

"Tomorrow afternoon," Gwenda said. Sarutha gave one sharp nod again. Gwenda gripped Maya's hand. "You come, too," she said, "okay?"

"Sure," said Maya. She had been in several apartments at Janus House, but she'd never visited Gwenda's. "Hey, do you guys celebrate Halloween? We're carving our pumpkins tomorrow."

"Halloween? That's a whole other subject," said Gwenda, and then Maya's mother said it was time to sing again, and everybody settled down except Candra, who went upstairs to get away from the ultimate dorkiness of group music.

# TWO

"Come on. She said it was okay," Maya told Candra the next afternoon as they approached the steps to Janus House's front porch.

"I know," said Candra. "I want to go inside. I've wanted to for a long time." Then she turned around and headed back to the sidewalk, away from the verandah that surrounded the big, complicated, old-fashioned building that held the Janus House Apartments and all sorts of hidden rooms and other secrets.

"Candra," Maya said. She grabbed her big sister's hand and dragged her toward the building again.

"This is what *always* happens when I try to come over here," Candra said. "Keep hanging on, will you?"

"Weird," said Maya. Candra was trying to pull free.

"Hey." Peter came up behind them. "If you guys are going to Janus House, I want to go, too."

Peter's fists were clenched at his sides, his eyebrows lowered, as he trudged up the path toward them. He got halfway there and suddenly turned around. "Hey."

*An energy reaches out and persuades their bodies they don't want to come here*, Rimi told Maya.

*The wards*, Maya thought. She'd heard her teachers and others mention warding the house against intruders, but she hadn't seen it work before.

*It reaches for their minds, too, but they are focused now, and harder to persuade.*

"You guys, wait here. I'll go get Gwenda," Maya said. She released Candra, who wandered away. Peter fidgeted on the pathway, frowning as he faced the house.

Maya crossed the porch and opened one of the double front doors. She stepped over the threshold into the foyer of the building.

Inside, the space opened into a broad, three-story entry with a special welcome-to-the-outside-world mat you wiped your feet on as you left the building. Janus House people had to be careful not to take the dust of other worlds where outsiders might sense it. Maya wasn't sure what her family would make of a doormat on the inside of the door. If anything. Heck. She didn't have to explain.

Benjamin's apartment was to the left as she entered. Wide stairs rose before her, and hallways led past the staircase on either side, with different colored apartment doors opening off them. Maya's teacher Sarutha's apartment was on the third floor, with its own tiny balcony, where they sat amid Sarutha's potted plants and drank tea sometimes while Maya was studying. Maya wasn't sure which door Gwenda lived behind.

She knocked on Benjamin's green door. A moment later, Benjamin answered, and she smiled at him. He smiled back. "Hi. Are we expecting you?"

"Gwenda said Candra could come over and see her closet today, only I don't know where Gwenda lives, and anyway, Candra can't seem to get to the house. How does that work?"

Benjamin frowned. "Oh, yeah. I bet Gwenda forgot about the wards."

"Peter wants to come, too. Is there a way for them to come in?"

"Sure." He turned and called toward the kitchen, "Hey,

Mom. It's Maya. I have to go out and let her sister and brother through the wards and take them to Gwenda's, okay?"

"Did Harper approve that?" Dr. Porta's voice was a little muffled.

Benjamin raised his eyebrows at Maya.

"Sarutha seemed to think it would be okay," Maya said.

"I'm going," Benjamin called to his mother, and then he stepped out of the apartment and closed the door behind him.

When Benjamin and Maya came out on the front porch, Candra and Peter were gone. Maya sighed. Benjamin followed her back to her house, across a carpet of grass. "Hey," Maya called as she and Benjamin came into the living room, "Peter? Candra?"

Both of them came out of the kitchen.

"What happened?"

"Like I said, what always happens when I try going there," Candra said. "I end up somewhere else."

"Let's try it again. I brought a native guide."

"Oh, yeah," Candra said, "the cute one. Hi, there."

Benjamin blushed.

"Candra, Benjamin. Benjamin, Candra." Maya was mad

at Candra for noticing, for saying "the cute one" aloud, and for making Benjamin uncomfortable.

"Hi, Benjamin," Peter said.

"Hi, Peter. Hey, you guys. *Hishlah*. Come on over."

*Hishlah,* thought Rimi. *Curious.*

This time Maya didn't have to drag Candra up the front path. She walked on her own, and almost crowded Maya and Benjamin off the path in her eagerness to get inside.

Peter rushed inside, too.

Both Maya's siblings paused in the front entry to stare. Maya, who had been coming here three days a week for a month and a half, blinked and tried to look at it with fresh eyes. The staircase had wide steps covered in warm red carpet that also covered the floor of the entryway and hallways, and the balusters were hand-carved with images of vines. Capping the newel posts at the bottom of the banisters were honey-colored wooden rings big enough to put your hand through. The hallways looked pretty normal, except the light fixtures were shaped like metal dragons holding balls of light. Light came from a skylight somewhere high above, aimed down by frosted mirrors.

"Wow," said Candra.

Maya wondered why she had never drawn the entryway.

She guessed maybe it was because the first time she'd come in, she'd felt so sick she couldn't focus, and the next few times she was rushing through to get somewhere else. Now it was too normal for her to notice.

"Gwenda lives upstairs," said Benjamin. He led them up to the second floor.

Two hallways led past a structure that was an extension of the downstairs central courtyard. Frosted glass let light in from that open space, but you couldn't see clearly through the windows. Sometimes aliens and strangers from other dimensions met there, so it was just as well.

Many of the rooms where the Janus House kids trained and practiced the magic skills associated with portal-keeping were on the second floor. Maya studied singing in the music room with the little kids, and also, privately, with Sarutha. Benjamin, Gwenda, and the other Janus House kids Maya's age had already advanced far beyond her skill in their musical studies, so they had different classes.

Maya also spent time in another classroom with the youngest kids, studying the principles behind portal magic. She had had to start at the beginning in magic principles, too. So she was friends with the seven five- and six-year-olds in the house, and embarrassed because they were so much better at magic than she was. She had no idea what Gwenda and Benjamin were actually studying.

Most of the training rooms Maya had visited were off the left-hand hall. Benjamin led them down the right-hand hall and stopped at the third door down, which was sky blue. He knocked.

Gwenda's older sister, Fiona, answered the door. She was tall and slender, with short red hair, light skin, and blue-green eyes. She was wearing jeans and a blue blouse with small white flowers on it. "Good afternoon," she said, eyebrows up.

"Hey," said Candra. "Aren't you in my botany class?"

"Candra," said Fiona. "Huh."

"We're here to see Gwenda's closet," Maya said.

"That's peculiar," said Fiona. "Gwenda!"

Gwenda joined her sister at the door. She was wearing jeans, too, and a yellow embroidered blouse. "Oh, hi! Peter, too?"

"I wanted to see. Is that okay?" Peter asked.

"Sure. I cleaned my room, so what the heck."

"Why are these people visiting your closet, Gwenda?" Fiona asked.

"I don't know. It was Candra's idea."

"*Aren't* you in my botany class?" Candra asked Fiona again.

"I suppose I am," Fiona said. "Fiona Janus." She held out a hand and Candra shook it.

"I didn't realize you lived here."

Fiona shrugged and wandered off.

"Come in," said Gwenda. "Mama? Here are my guests."

Vivian Janus rose from a couch in the living room. Her coloring was like Gwenda's—dark hair and blue eyes—and she had the same high cheekbones and clean beauty. She wore a complicated green dress made of panels of overlapping material, with a gold sash tied at the waist. She set down something she had been knitting. It looked long and tubular, like a sleeve, only it was bigger than any Earth arm. "So nice to see you," she said, smiling at all of them. "Welcome to our home, Maya, Peter. This is your sister?"

"Yes. This is Candra Andersen, Mama," Gwenda said. "Candra, my mother, Vivian Janus."

Maya looked past Gwenda's mother. This living room looked different from the others she had seen in Janus House Apartments. The furniture looked elegant and mostly had spindly legs, with fringed pillows covered in blue and white material arranged on off-white upholstered couches and chairs. A glass-topped table with curly ironwork legs stood on layers of fancy carpets. The apartment smelled like incense. Most Janus House residents seemed to burn things that changed the way the air smelled.

"Nice to meet you, Ms. Janus. What a nice place you have," Candra said.

"Thank you," said Ms. Janus. Her smiled showed a dimple in her right cheek. "I try."

"Candra wanted to see my clothes, Mama," Gwenda said.

"Anyone would. Please come in." Ms. Janus stood aside for them to enter. "Would you like some tea?"

Candra glanced in all directions. Maya looked, too, trying to see what Candra was seeing, or at least figure out what she was searching for. Candra had made remarks at supper a few times about the possibility of Janus House people belonging to weird religious cults and sacrificing babies, until Dad told her to stop that. "Andersens do not indulge in bad-mouthing people we don't know," he had said. "Or those we do."

There were no obvious clues to the magical nature of the people who lived here, Maya thought. It wasn't like they had pentacles or brooms or bloody axes hanging from the wall.

"Tea?" Candra said to Gwenda's mother. "What kinds do you have?"

Peter nudged her. "Tea would be nice, Ms. Janus. Thanks for the offer."

Wild that Peter had better manners than Candra, thought Maya. Especially when Candra had started out so uncharacteristically polite. Maybe she had forgotten she was on a fact-finding mission and acted like her true self by mistake.

Maya also wondered what kind of tea they had. Janus House specialized in peculiar beverages, some of which had strange side effects.

"We have many sorts," Ms. Janus said. "I'll make you some chamomile."

Candra hated chamomile. She opened her mouth, and Peter kicked her in the shin. "Uh, thanks," she said, glaring at Peter.

He smiled up at her. It was not a nice smile.

*The picture of power is over the couch*, Rimi thought.

Maya looked at the framed artwork over the couch. Every Janus House apartment she'd been in had some picture or knickknack that the inhabitants could touch to contact each other. They seemed to work like walkie-talkies.

Maybe phones didn't work in Janus House. She already knew that her cell phone didn't, but she'd seen people using handheld communicators made of what looked like wire mesh.

This communications picture was of a man playing a harp, and Maya had critical thoughts about it. The palette was sour. The man was wearing a yellow shirt. Through the harp you could see dark blue sky. There were red velvet curtains to the sides of the picture. The man's hair was carroty, and his pants were green. It was an ugly picture that didn't go with the rest of the delicate, elegant furnishings.

*They're all ugly, those power pictures,* Rimi thought. Maya wondered if Rimi shared Maya's taste or had her own ideas of how things should look. Maya wasn't sure how Rimi even saw, a shadow without eyes, but Rimi had shared enough of her visions that Maya knew she saw somehow.

*What does it look like to you?* she thought.

A shadow dropped over Maya's eyes, and she saw glowing brown and purple and green pinpricks knotted together in a sullen mass.

*Yuck. You're right. I wonder why they're like that?* She glanced around the room through Rimi's enhanced vision, noticed Gwenda looked like Gwenda except for the glows of her bracelet. Vivian had a green glowing throat, and Benjamin—his hands had golden gloves of glow. *Rimi? What's that about?*

*People wear their power. You don't see it?*

*No. Not like this.*

*Tell me when you want to see it like this, and I'll help you.*

*Thanks, Rimi.* Maya thought about the drawings she'd work on when she got home. She had several sketch pads hidden in her room. Some she could share with her family, and others were private studies just for herself, and a few others were things she wanted to show the Janus House people. She was still finding images in her mind from Rimi's first bondmate, Bikos, who had died just as school began. When she could, she drew pictures of Bikos's memories. Bikos had spent some time on the Krithi planet, and everybody involved in portal traffic wanted to know more about the Krithi. *Okay, I'm ready to go back to my own vision now.*

The shadow lifted from her eyes, and everything looked normal again. The power picture was still ugly.

Gwenda's mother had gone into the kitchen to make the tea, presumably. Gwenda smiled brightly and said, "Would you like to come to my room?"

"Sure," said Candra.

Gwenda led them down a hall that passed two doorways before she turned in at the third doorway. Her room had a bed, a dresser, a chair, and a desk—more furniture with feet that seemed too small to support the rest of it, let alone if someone actually sat on the chair, leaned on the desk, or lay on the bed. The furniture was white with gold lines, and the bed had flounces.

Maya was more interested in the walls. Gwenda had made a collage of photographs, some big, some small, all arranged into a beautiful mosaic of colorful people and places: an empty stretch of red desert with tall square rock formations in the distance, a lively marketplace midstream on boats, a winter landscape of snowy expanses with dark pine trees, people wearing heavy hide coats and colorful knitted caps and gloves. There was a white-sand island with palm trees and turquoise water, and high, stark white mountaintop ruins under burning blue skies. Everywhere Maya looked, she saw another intriguing place or person.

"Wow," she said.

Gwenda glanced around, then lifted her hands. "Still working on it," she said. "I got most of the pictures from old calendars and magazines, but a few are photographs people in my family took."

"Very, very cool," said Maya.

"Do you know this kid?" Peter asked, pointing to a little boy with dark skin who smiled wide enough to show a two-tooth gap. He stood in front of a hut that looked like it was made of dried red-brown mud and straw, and he held up a stick with ribbons wound around it.

"It's my cousin Sipho," Gwenda said. She smiled at the picture of the little boy.

"Did you take the picture?" Peter asked.

"My dad did, in Africa."

"Neat." Peter leaned forward, staring at the lower corner of the picture. "Whoa. Look at that. There's a Goliath beetle! How cool is that?"

*All these pictures glow a little*, Rimi said.

*May I see?* Maya asked.

A flicker of shadow and she saw that colors like the bright ones around the stones of Gwenda's bracelet lay over these pictures, very thin, like gauze scarves, but everywhere. Maya nodded, and Rimi's shadow-view vanished.

Gwenda opened the closet door, turned on a light, and stood back. She gestured toward the closet and nodded to Candra and Maya.

Candra pushed past Gwenda and stood in the closet. "Whoa," she said. "How do you rate a clothes budget like this?"

Maya peeked in. The closet was bigger than hers, with hanger bars on both sides, and lots of colorful dresses, skirts, and blouses on hangers.

"I have these friends. They're, like, my clothes pals instead of my pen pals. Instead of letters, we send each other clothes. They live on the other side of the world. This skirt is from my friend Pavlína in Prague, and that shirt is from Fahima in Cairo. I send them American clothes I get in thrift stores, and they send me stuff they find in second-hand shops."

"Awesome," said Candra. She slid hangers sideways, pausing to study embroidered shirts, pleated skirts, gypsy vests.

"I get better stuff than my friends do, I think." Gwenda smiled.

"Boy howdy." Candra knelt to peer at the shoes lined up below the clothes. There were only five pairs. Gwenda's favorite knee-high red leather boots were there, and a pair of narrow leather ankle-high shoes that laced up. Gwenda didn't seem to own any tennis shoes. "Could you introduce me to your friends?"

Gwenda sighed. "That would be hard. I could lend you some of my clothes."

Candra straightened. She was five inches taller than

Gwenda, and she had a bust. Gwenda was pretty straight up and down. Some of the clothes were loose, though, and a lot of the skirts gathered at the waist with ties.

"That would be great," Candra said.

Peter was working his way around the room, still studying the photographs. He muttered to himself whenever he saw a new animal.

"So that's the secret of my closet. Are you happy now?" asked Gwenda.

"Happier than I was," said Candra, "but not all the way happy. Thanks for showing me, anyway."

"You're welcome," Gwenda said, and then her mother came to the door and announced that tea was ready.

Ms. Janus led them back through the living room and into the kitchen, where there was a large, circular table they could all fit around. Fiona nodded to them from the living room couch but didn't join them.

The kitchen looked disappointingly normal. It had a white stove, a white refrigerator, pale gold countertops, wooden cupboards, and a stainless steel sink. The teakettle on the stove was red and still steaming. A brown clay teapot and some teacups sat on the table near one of the straight-backed chairs. A white plate held pale brown cookies that looked pretty darned generic.

A gold-skinned stranger stood by the counter, shaking sugar from a box into a sugar bowl. He looked up as they came in and flashed a smile. He had curly blond hair and green eyes. He was tall, slender, and handsome, and he wore a green shirt with a black leather vest over it. His jeans and boots were also black.

*Who is that?* Maya thought. He had a look that reminded her of Benjamin, but she didn't think she had seen him before. She would have sketched him if she had; she liked how he looked.

*It's Evren,* Rimi thought. *He comes to your house every Saturday night. You never noticed him before?*

*No,* Maya thought. She had never seen him before, she was pretty sure, because she was always studying people at Music Night. If someone had been there every time, and she hadn't noticed him—

*He is strange. That's why I watch him. He sings, but no one seems to hear him, and nobody ever talks to him. He looks around a lot. I like watching him. He moves past people and they don't even seem to know.*

*He's invisible!* Maya thought. *But we can see him now?*

*I can always see him, but invisible would explain why other people don't notice him. Hmm,* Rimi thought. *He has always been* twizzly, *and no one else has been.*

"Well, hi, there." Candra flashed her own wide smile.

Ms. Janus said, "Candra, this is—"

"Cousin Evren?" Gwenda said. Maya glanced at her. Gwenda looked astonished.

"That's right," said Ms. Janus. "Evren Janus, Candra Andersen."

"A great pleasure." Evren took Candra's hand. He didn't shake it, just held it and stared into Candra's eyes, his smile never slipping.

"And Maya Andersen and Peter Andersen," Ms. Janus said.

"Of course," said Evren. He finally released Candra's hand and turned to share his smile with Maya and Peter. "Nice to meet you." He winked at Maya.

"Hi," she said. If a guy was invisible all the time and over at her house, he probably felt like he knew her, but she didn't know him. Weird.

"Evren's going to join us for tea," said Ms. Janus.

"Right, I was just getting down the sugar." Evren finished filling the sugar bowl and put away the box. He brought the sugar bowl to the table. "Cream, Viv?"

"Yes, please," said Ms. Janus.

Evren got a carton of half-and-half out of the refrigerator, poured some into a creamer, and added it to the array of dishes on the table. Everybody sat down. Evren sat between Candra and Ms. Janus.

The chamomile tea was pretty nasty. Maya added sugar and cream to drown the flavor. She and Rimi both watched for side effects and didn't find any.

The cookies looked plain vanilla and tasted like licorice.

"So, Evren, how old are you?" Candra asked. She had touched her lips to her teacup, but she hadn't actually drunk any of it.

"How old do you think I am?"

"No fair," said Candra. "Either I guess right, or you're insulted. Give it up, buddy."

"I'm nineteen. How old are you?"

"Seventeen. Are you going away to college?"

"Not this year." He smiled at her.

"So you're hanging around here? What do you people find to do all day?"

"We work," said Evren.

"Work at what?" Candra asked.

"Most of us are in the family import-export business. Many of us work out of our homes."

"My clothes pals' parents are part of our business," Gwenda said.

"You guys ship clothes around the world?"

"Clothes, other goods, passengers. We facilitate various kinds of travel," said Evren.

"Could you get me to Europe?" Candra asked.

Evren frowned, and Ms. Janus shook her head. "Our clientele is pretty specialized," she said. "We might be able to help you arrange a trip—"

"But not any better than Travelocity or Expedia," Evren said.

"Too bad," said Candra.

The talk turned to trips people had taken. They ate all the cookies. There was lots of tea left.

"Welp," said Candra eventually, "we've got innocent pumpkins to murder or deface." She stood up. "Nice to meet you. Thanks for showing me your closet, Gwenda."

"Thanks for your hospitality," Peter said to Ms. Janus.

"You're welcome. It's a pleasure to have a visit from such a gentleman," said Ms. Janus.

"You're Bran's mother, right?" Peter asked.

"Yes, I am."

"He's in my class at school. He's kind of hard to talk to, though."

"I know what you mean."

"Would you tell him I'm not his enemy?"

"Sure, Peter. Or you could tell him yourself." She crossed the living room, headed down the hall, and knocked on the first door. "Bran!"

"What?" said a grumpy voice.

"We have visitors."

"I know. That's why I'm hiding."

Ms. Janus turned to them and shrugged.

"Oh, well," said Peter. He waved and they left. Gwenda came down the stairs with them and outside.

"*Lahish*," Gwenda murmured as they crossed the lawn toward the Andersens' house.

*Interesting*, thought Rimi.

"So, like Candra said, we're having a pumpkin carving party now," Maya said to Gwenda. "Do you want to come? We don't have a pumpkin for you, but you could help me with mine."

"That's all right, Maya. I don't know if I want to watch people torturing vegetables." She smiled. "It's not part of our tradition."

"You wouldn't tell me last night whether you guys celebrate Halloween."

"It's an interesting time of year," Gwenda said.

"Why's that?" asked Candra.

"People say ghosts walk on that night, and the walls between the universes are thinner. You can see strange things you don't see other times of year."

"Neat," said Peter.

"Do you believe things like that?" Candra asked.

"I'm not sure." Gwenda frowned. "I haven't met any ghosts, but I've talked to people who say they have."

"Double neat," said Peter. "What was it like?"

"You'd have to ask them. I can't describe it well enough."

"Forget that," Maya said. "Do you guys dress up for Halloween? Do you trick-or-treat?" Maya wasn't sure when you were too old to trick-or-treat. Stephanie had said she wanted to keep doing it until she was twenty-one. "Face it," Steph had said, "when else can you run around being scary and get candy for it? Why ever give this up?"

Maya got the crushed-glass-against-your-skin shiver she felt whenever she thought of Steph's future plans. Then she shook her head and looked at Gwenda, who was here now, and alive.

"Some of the little kids dress up because their classes at school are doing it, but we're not supposed to, really," Gwenda said. "We're supposed to just stay home. I'd like to go trick-or-treating sometime."

"This year," Maya said. "Come with me."

Gwenda looked into Maya's eyes. Rimi sent out a tendril and teased a lock of Gwenda's hair, and Gwenda, the first person besides Maya to meet Rimi when Rimi hatched, smiled. "Maybe I will."

# THREE

Monday morning the alarm shrilled, and Maya woke and stared at the ceiling. Yesterday she'd been up to her arms in seeds and pumpkin slime, slinging strings of pumpkin guts at Peter and Candra in the kitchen, and now she had to go back to normal life. School.

Her shadow rose and stretched into a vaguely humanoid shape against the air. It waved at Maya.

Her shadow. Rimi, her alien friend who was part of her. Normal would probably never happen again.

"Good morning to you, too," Maya said. She sat up and glared at the clock.

Rimi went to the closet, opened it, and pulled out a green shirt with a frog on the front.

"I guess," Maya said. She stood, shucked off her night-gown, and held out her arms. The shadow brought her the shirt, and she put it on. "I'm not sure I should be letting you make my fashion choices."

*I see you more than you do, Mayamela,* Rimi thought.

"But your eyes are different," said Maya.

*I like to like what I'm looking at.*

"You have a point. But a lot of other people are look-ing at me, too, and—heck with it." Maya pulled on under-wear and jeans. She put on socks and shoes, then shoved her sketchbook and pencil case into her backpack. She turned toward the door.

*You're forgetting something,* Rimi thought.

"Huh? Oh, yeah." Maya headed back to her desk and picked up her homework, school notebook, and textbooks and added them to the pack. "Thanks."

She opened her door and found Peter standing in the upstairs hall. He turned and raced for the stairs. "Mom! Maya's talking to herself again!" he yelled as he clattered down the stairs ahead of her.

"That's allowed," said their mother. "You do it, too."

"But she's having whole conversations," Peter said. "I just mutter."

"Shut up, brat. Why were you listening at my door?

Don't you have better things to do? Anyway, we're allowed to do whatever we like in our own rooms as long as it doesn't destroy anything or hurt anyone." Maya pushed past Peter and scooped oatmeal out of a pot on the stove and into a bowl, added milk, raisins, and brown sugar. She ate standing up.

"Maya, who were you talking to?" Mom asked.

"My shadow," said Maya.

Mom turned to Peter. "What's wrong with that?"

Peter looked at Maya's shadow. Rimi waved a shadow arm at him, and he jumped.

*Stop it, Rimi!* Maya thought. *We're not allowed to let anyone else know about you!*

Rimi settled into a distorted monochrome version of Maya, hunched over the bowl she held. *I'm tired of being a secret,* Rimi thought. *I want to play with Peter.*

*It's not my decision,* Maya thought.

"Mom, did you see—" Peter began. "No, of course you didn't."

"It's time to go, Peter," Mom said. "Grab your stuff."

Peter took his lunch and backpack and followed Mom out the backdoor to her car. They were off to elementary school, where Peter studented and Mom taught.

Maya glanced at the clock. She had ten minutes to run

to middle school and settle into her chair in the back row of Mr. Ferrell's homeroom. She dumped the rest of her oatmeal into Sully the golden retriever's food bowl, put it out on the back porch next to his water dish, then rinsed out her bowl and stuck it in the dishwasher. Her father and Candra had already left for the high school. Everybody scattered in the morning.

Maya's shadow clumped over the food in Sully's bowl before Sully could get to it. Maya felt ripples in her stomach as Rimi absorbed the oatmeal. Maya shimmied her shoulders to shake off a shudder. She was still getting used to Rimi's new form and the things it did. Rimi wasn't really a shadow; she liked to eat. She didn't have much substance, though. Sometimes what she ate went straight to Maya's stomach, or, worse, into Maya's mouth, where Maya had to taste it. Rimi liked tasting things that weren't food, and she was all about sharing the experience. Sometimes that was a good thing; Rimi tasted clouds, butterfly-wing dust, fire, happiness. Sometimes it was just dreadful, to the point where Maya had to throw up. Rimi had learned to edit what she shared. Sometimes.

Today Rimi was probably eating because she thought Maya needed to eat.

Maya pulled on her coat and backpack, grabbed the

lunch she'd packed the night before, and ran out the front door. She dashed for school, right past Janus House, without stopping to say hello to Sarutha, who was sitting on the verandah with her backstrap loom attached to one of the posts. The teacher often sat facing the street, working on projects whose uses Maya was just beginning to learn. Maya waved and ran. She'd see Sarutha after school.

Maya slowed as she ran past a store called Dreams & Bones. It was a bookstore/comic store/anime DVD rental/ café only a block and a half from home. Peter loved it. Maya had been inside several times before school started, but never since. She liked the anime and movie tie-in toys, and she loved paging through the manga and comic books, but she was scared of the proprietor. He looked about fifty, tall, thin, and wiry. He wore his long black hair in a braid down his back, had intense black eyes under craggy brows, and dressed in dark, nondescript clothing. Every time he stared toward her, Maya had felt sad and strange, and she didn't know why. And he kept studying her, more, she thought, than he watched the other customers. Maybe he thought she was shoplifting? She couldn't tell. Still, it made her uncomfortable.

Even though the store was full of wonderful creamy-colored wooden shelves crowded with things she could have spent hours looking at, she stayed away after those first few visits.

*I want,* Rimi thought as Maya peeked in through the window. The café part was up front, five small tables with ladder-backed chairs grouped around them. Part of the window showed the inside of the pastry case, with dough-nuts and Danishes laid in rows on paper doily–topped trays. The store wasn't open yet, but yellow light glowed in the back, where the books were.

*Want what?* Maya wondered. She hadn't gone into Dreams & Bones since she and Rimi had bonded.

*Don't know. Inside that place—some kind of energy. A taste I tasted before. I* sisti *strange flavors. Want to explore.*

*Later,* Maya thought. She ran on to school.

Students milled in front of Hoover Middle School. The building was all yellow brick and wide windows. Parents pulled up, and students slammed out of cars without a back-ward glance. First bell hadn't rung yet, apparently. Maya glanced at her watch, which definitely said eight fifteen. She should be in homeroom by now. "Hey, Helen," she called to a red-haired girl she knew from language arts class. "What time is it?"

Helen got out her cell phone and checked. "Ten past eight."

Dad must have sneaked through the house and set all the clocks and watches five minutes fast. He did this every once in a while. It always made Maya mad, but then she was glad when she actually got where she should be on time. "Thanks," she yelled, and ran into the building. Belatedly, she pulled out her own cell phone. She hadn't had it long enough to be used to it. When she opened it, it asked her whether it should update the time. She pressed the YES button and saw that according to the gods of cell phone timing, it was still eight ten, as Helen had said. She turned off the phone, shoved it back in her pocket, and headed down the hall to her classroom.

After settling in her seat in the back of homeroom, she took off her watch and reset it, three minutes fast instead of five.

*You could ask me what time it is,* Rimi said.

*How would you know?* Maya thought.

*Time weaves through most things here. There are different times here and there, but I can find the right stream.*

*Okay. Next time I'll ask you. Could you be an alarm clock? Wake you at a specific time? Of course,* Rimi thought.

*Whoa. Gotta think about that, but coolness.* Maya strapped her watch on and glanced sideways at Benjamin, in the desk to her left.

Today he was wearing a black hoodie with thin white lines wandering over it. Up close, it looked like a topographical map, but from a distance, it looked gray, which was how Maya felt about Benjamin. If you didn't look hard, you might not notice how interesting he was.

"Hey," she muttered.

"Hi," he said, and then, *"Ke dey ee dun?"* How have you been?

*"Shtru,"* she said, which meant *okay.* Part of her training was learning Kerlinqua.

She leaned forward to peer past Benjamin at Gwenda. Gwenda was wearing a red skirt with straw-yellow petticoats that made it stand out. It was hemmed with lace. She had on a pale yellow shirt and wore a dark green webwork jacket over it. She waved one finger at Maya and smiled, shaking her charm bracelet.

"All right, people, settle down. Answer when I call your name," said Mr. Ferrell from up front.

Maya got out her sketchbook and a couple of soft lead pencils. Mr. Ferrell called her name, Andersen, almost first, so she could focus on drawing while he went down the rest of the list. She sketched the row of chairs in front of her, adding the people sitting in them after she'd gotten good outlines of the furniture.

She was concentrating on getting just the right shine in Helen's red-blonde hair when Benjamin hissed at her. She glanced at him, and he nodded toward her sketch pad, where another of her pencils was moving across her drawing, flowing in faint shadows below the chairs in the picture.

# FOUR

Maya cocked her head and watched Rimi add to her drawing. Would Maya have drawn those same shadows? She wasn't sure. Teamwork shifted the focus of the picture. Maybe that made it better. Rimi was skilled, with a wonderful flow of line and evenness of pressure that made her shadows look sculpted. Maya hadn't seen Rimi draw before.

Maya wanted Rimi to draw a picture from scratch. Rimi had a lot of strange senses Maya didn't even have names for. Maya could borrow Rimi's sight (how *did* Rimi see?) and taste (yuck!) and sometimes even smell (the world was full of things that smelled awful when you got close to them!).

They hadn't shared other senses yet. Obviously Rimi saw shadows, but what about the rest of it?

Benjamin hissed again, and Maya grabbed Rimi's pencil, then looked up. A girl a couple of rows in front of them had turned and was staring back at her. It was Sibyl Katsaros, a slender dark-haired girl with glasses that magnified her gray-green eyes. She was wearing a green dress, when most of the girls in the room wore jeans, and she had a golden scarf wrapped around her neck.

Maya smiled and shrugged. She hadn't spoken with Sibyl in school yet. Gwenda had warned Maya when Maya first sat with the Janus House kids that being with them would kill her chance at a normal social life, but Maya figured the benefits outweighed the risks.

Sibyl lowered her eyebrows and the corners of her mouth into a ferocious frown and faced forward again.

"So is she the enemy now?" Maya whispered to Benjamin.

"She moved here around the same time you did," Benjamin whispered back. "Rowan thinks there's something strange about her. But also, you're not supposed to act up in public."

"It wasn't me," Maya said.

Benjamin lifted one eyebrow. Maya hated that. She couldn't do it, and she really wanted to. "It might not be you," he whispered, "but it's your responsibility."

"You're such a jerk sometimes," Maya said.

Benjamin flinched.

"Well, so am I," Maya said. "Like right now. Don't go all Rowan on me."

"Sorry," Benjamin whispered. He looked away. Then he turned back. "She's been watching us since she moved here. I feel like we need to be careful around her. You don't know our history yet. We've had break-ins before."

"Break-ins?" Maya repeated.

"People who break into our lives, find out stuff they shouldn't, and want to do something bad with that knowledge. All through our history, which stretches back pretty far, we've had break-ins. Once in a while it works out. Sometimes security takes action that's too drastic, and we have to leave and start over somewhere else. We do it if we have to, but we'd much rather not. It's a lot of work! Trust me when I tell you, everything works better when we keep our secrets secret."

"Okay, I get it," Maya muttered. *Rimi?*

She felt a sort of stretch through her connection to Rimi,

as though her shadow were taffy being dragged out between two fists. *I want to play.*

*I understand,* Maya thought. *We'll go to the woods after school. No, we have to go for training. Well, you can play at Janus House.*

Rimi did a mental shimmy, her equivalent of a shrug with prejudice. *They're scared of me there.*

*Really?* Maya hadn't noticed anybody at Janus House running in fear. Usually she felt so overwhelmed with that jangling feeling of my-whole-world-is-upside-down in the presence of people who used magic on a regular basis that she never noticed if they were scared of her. *I wonder what we can do to—*

Tall, blond, long-haired Travis Finnegan edged into class and made his way to his usual seat to her right. He wasn't being loud about it, but it was hard to ignore the biggest kid in the class, and the only one on his feet. "Third tardy this week," Mr. Ferrell said, marking his attendance sheet. "That's detention, Travis."

Travis groaned. "I can't do detention," he muttered. "What about my training?" Travis was training at Janus House, too, only he was training as a human helper. He didn't go to singing class or principles of magic.

"Why were you late?" Maya whispered.

"Oma needed extra help in the bathroom this morning after Dad left. That keeps happening. The day care woman, Ms. Ringo, she gets there just before I leave, and Oma needs help sooner than that."

Maya touched his hand. His grandmother had been hurt in the car crash that killed his grandfather a little more than a year ago, and since that time, Travis and his father had lived with Travis's grandmother. Travis was an important part of his grandmother's care team. Some things were more important than school. Which was why Travis had flunked seventh grade last year.

Travis smiled tiredly, got his social studies textbook out of his pack, and opened it to a historic map of the United States. "Harrison's going to give us another quiz disguised as a game today, isn't he?" Travis said.

"That's the rumor," said Maya.

*I could find out*, Rimi thought.

*How?* asked Maya.

*I could stretch.* Rimi flexed, which Maya felt more than saw, and then a faint, faint shadow raced across the floor, one end still anchored under Maya's feet, the other zipping up the aisle between desks and under the door, with no one else noticing.

Maya felt Rimi's stretch the same way she sometimes

tasted what Rimi tasted; she sensed the scuffed surface of the hallway linoleum as Rimi stretched and stretched, an almost invisible finger of self, to dive under the door in the social studies classroom where Mr. Harrison was talking to his homeroom class. Rimi felt the vibration of voices in the air above, but didn't shape herself into the kind of surface that could decode the sounds; hearing was a sense she employed often, but not always. The shadow arrowed across the floor and climbed up the teacher's desk's leg, then slid across the top of the desk to the stack of papers under Mr. Harrison's hand.

Mr. Harrison was focused on his attendance sheet, vibrating the air with his voice. Maya wasn't sure how she knew what he was doing or where he was focused; they weren't looking with eyes as Maya understood them.

Rimi's edge of self spread across the surfaces of the papers under Mr. Harrison's hands and the attendance sheet. Maya felt the flicker of something printing against Rimi's surface, then another flicker of confused impressions as Rimi shifted to another page, then another. Rimi's shadow self could slip from page to page without lifting a corner.

Moments later the shadow withdrew as swiftly and silently as it had gone out, snapping back to its central core under Maya's feet.

"What did we learn?" Maya muttered.

*Wait*, Rimi thought. A growling in Maya's stomach echoed some inner processing Rimi was doing, and then Maya was seeing what the pages looked like, including the quiz Mr. Harrison had written for today's class, along with his lecture notes, a couple of visuals he was going to use with the day's lectures, and a letter to his girlfriend in Hawaii.

# FIVE

"Oh, no," she said. "No, Rimi."

"What's she doing now?" Benjamin asked.

Maya swallowed and closed her eyes. She could still see the pages on the insides of her eyelids. "Make them go away," she said, but she couldn't help skimming.

Rimi whisked the images away. Maya rubbed her eyes. The usual explosion of purple stars splashed the darkness inside her eyelids, and she let out a breath she hadn't known she was holding.

*We can know,* Rimi thought.

*But we shouldn't,* Maya thought.

Benjamin poked her. "What?" he asked.

Maya opened her eyes and glanced at him. She was supposed to tell him, or one of the Janus House kids, everything that happened between her and Rimi. Gwenda and Benjamin were the ones she trusted most, but she knew they answered to a lot of other people in the house, some of whom she didn't trust.

Rimi was a *sissimi*, a species alien to Earth. Janus House people ran into species alien to Earth every day in the course of running their portal. Still, they hadn't had much experience with *sissimi*.

*Sissimi* could bond with any known species, and their bonds were different with every match.

Maya and Rimi were closer to each other than family— Rimi called their bond Second Family, First Family being Maya's parents and siblings (because they were Maya's family first), and Third Family being the Janus House folk who had adopted Maya and Rimi after Rimi hatched.

Rimi and Maya were part of each other, and Maya figured they might need to keep some of their own secrets.

On the other hand, dangerous secrets needed to be shared. Janus House people could help with things no one in Maya's own family would understand. She could get into trouble she couldn't even anticipate. . . .

Benjamin nudged her again. "Maya? Are you all right?"

"Yeah," she said, and then the bell rang and they rose to go to their next class. "Tell you later."

Outside the classroom, Maya and Travis headed one direction, and Benjamin and Gwenda another.

Travis walked down the corridor in a fog, and kids moved out of his way. Maya had never seen him hurt anyone, but people seemed to respect or fear him. He was a good buddy to have in a crowded hallway.

They crossed the yard between buildings and made it to Ms. Caras's language arts just before second bell. It was one of the classes Travis and Maya had without any Janus House kids in it, and they sat toward the front in this one, though still next to each other.

It was Maya's first year at Hoover, and she was still finding her way. She looked around at the other students. They'd all done essays about their summers during the first week of Ms. Caras's class, so she knew a little about them. Helen, the one who used her cell phone as a watch, sat to Maya's left. Maya thought she might make a good friend. Even though Maya now had Rimi, Travis, Benjamin, Gwenda, and a host of other people living in Janus House as friends, she could use someone normal.

Helen returned her glance and half a smile.

"Do you know what you're going to be for Halloween?" Maya whispered to her.

Helen frowned. "My mom says I'm too old."

"Harsh."

During the pumpkin carving the day before, Mom and Dad had asked Candra if she was going to trick-or-treat this year, and Candra had said, "Nobody I know at school is doing it. They say if you're old enough to drive, you're too old to trick-or-treat. I wish I could go, though."

"You could escort Maya and Peter," Mom said.

"Oh, *Mom*," Peter moaned.

"Think of it as doing your big sister a favor," Mom told Peter. "She wants to go, and you're giving her a good reason."

"I think I should stay home and hand out the candy this year," Candra had said. She stabbed the knife into her pumpkin's mouth-line.

"Tell us how you really feel," said Dad, half teasing.

They had finished carving with Candra still not sure what she was going to do on Halloween.

Maya was going trick-or-treating no matter what Candra did. She wasn't sure what costume to wear yet, though. It had been a very confusing year; she didn't know what secret self she wanted to manifest this year.

*What am I going as?* Rimi asked.

Maya sat back, startled. She hadn't even thought about Rimi and Halloween. *Maybe I should go as you*, she thought.

*What would that look like?*

*Let's think about it!*

"What are you going as?" Helen whispered to Maya.

"I'm kind of vague on the details, but I just got an idea. If you *could* go, what would you be?"

"Last year I was a robot," muttered Helen. "I loved making that costume! And I could make a much better one this year."

Ms. Caras rapped on her desk with a yardstick. Today she was wearing her green cat's-eye glasses and a green dress with white dots, and she had her dark curls tied up but not completely subdued at the back of her neck.

"Okay, kids," she said. "This week we're going to write ghost stories! I want you to think about and practice generating suspense, so we'll start with a few exercises about that today, and I'll give you a list of vocabulary words to include in your story. Keep in mind that you're going to put together a ghost story by the end of this week. The first thing you need to figure out is who's dead and why they would come back to haunt someone, and the second thing is who's going to run into your ghost and why?"

*Ghosts,* thought Maya. Gwenda had talked about the wall between the worlds being thin on Halloween.

*Ghosts,* Rimi said. *I want to know more about ghosts.*

Maya raised her hand.

"Maya?" Ms. Caras said, surprised.

"Can you tell us more about ghosts? I mean, I've seen them on TV and in movies and books, but there are a lot of different kinds, and it seems like they can do different things. What are the ghost rules?"

"This is fiction, Maya, so you can make your own rules. There are lots of resources in the library and online if you want to learn more. I don't think there's one set of ghost rules. If you find one, could you bring it in to share with the class?"

Maya sat back, frustrated.

"So. Suspense. It's all about the details. . . ."

# SIX

"Field trip after school today," Benjamin told the kids at the Janus House table during lunch.

Maya had started out school sitting with the Janus House kids for lunch, and she still did, since they were most of the people she saw every day. She looked over at Helen's table. Helen was sitting with two other girls Maya had seen but didn't know. No, one of them was that girl Sibyl from homeroom. Sibyl had some kind of diet drink she was sipping, and she didn't seem to be talking much. Once in a while she looked over at Maya and narrowed her eyes. What was that about?

Travis sat with the Janus House kids some of the time,

but today he was over with his eighth-grade buddies. He had flunked seventh grade, but they still liked him.

"Where are we going this time?" Benjamin's older sister Twyla asked.

"Sviv," said Benjamin.

"Again?" Twyla made a face. "The air tastes terrible there. It gives me a sore throat."

"Uncle Dylan arranged for medical tutors to meet us," Benjamin said.

"Are you guys going through the portal?" Maya asked. She had seen the portal operate a number of times, but she hadn't seen any of the kids go through it. Mostly she'd seen otherworld travelers come and go. She liked watching them when she had a sketchbook and pencils in hand. Those were the sketchbooks she had to leave at Janus House.

"Yep," Benjamin said. "The Elders want us to meet teachers and get experience on other worlds. This is a short trip, just a few hours. Want to come? You've got to come sometime."

*NO!* Rimi thought. *No!*

*Ow, my head,* Maya thought, and aloud she said, "I think Rimi is allergic to portals."

"There'd better be some way to get her over that,"

Rowan said, scowling as usual. "If you're going to be one of us, you have to travel."

*No, no, no!* Rimi yelled, softer this time, but still emphatic.

"Maybe not this time," Benjamin said. "Twyla's right. Sviv isn't the funnest place to go on your first trip through the portal. Talk to Aunt Sarutha. She'll help you find a good place. Your first time should be great. Maybe she can track the trade missions and send you on one of those; you see the coolest things in the marketplaces."

A sketching tour, Maya thought. More pictures she wouldn't be able to take home, but seeing things and capturing them on paper carried its own reward. It was Maya's kind of magic.

*No portals,* Rimi said.

*What if we could go back to your home planet? The growing house where you were on a vine?* Maya had images of Rimi's home planet from when she had shared Bikos's memories. The thick, muscular *sissimi* vines had twisted through a hot, humid, glass-enclosed place, with glowing fruit hanging among the hand-shaped blue and purple leaves. *Find your relatives? Wouldn't you like that?*

Rimi thought of her seedhood in that warm place, where she and the other seeds were thinking together with the conscious parts of the vines and leaves that bore them and fed them. They stretched out under the ground with the rootnet, and reached toward light above them, and they had many, many thoughts. Some shared memories of ancient vines who had lived out under the open skies, those who had made first contact with otherworlders. Some remembered legends and myths, and others held memories of bonds the seeds had made with many offworlders. Rimi knew many things rested in the root minds, to be shared when the time came, and she knew she had left too soon, before she had learned all of them.

She shifted against Maya's skin, agitated. *I want to go home,* she said, *but not through a portal.*

*I don't think there's any other way. You've been through Krithi portals. We've seen the one at Janus House, and that one looks different. Maybe it feels different, too.*

*I'll think about it,* Rimi thought.

"We're not going through a portal today," Maya said.

Gwenda said, "I think they're planning something else for you today anyway."

"What do you mean?" Benjamin asked her.

"Aunt Sarutha was talking about inviting a new *sissimi* pair to visit and talk with Maya and Rimi."

"Oh!" Maya said. *Rimi! Someone to see you!*

*Good*, thought Rimi. *They will see how beautiful and perfect I am*. She had a smile in her thoughts.

*Yes, they will*, Maya thought.

*And I will learn more ways to make you safe. And more ways for me to have fun.*

# SEVEN

"Is Travis going on the field trip?" Maya asked when school let out and all the Janus House kids, plus Maya, Rimi, and Travis, headed for the apartment building.

"I don't think he's ready," said Benjamin.

Rowan said, "He can go if he can pass the tests."

"What field trip?" Travis asked.

"They're going on a field trip through the portal," said Maya. "Today."

"We do it about once a month," Benjamin said. "You should probably come on one soon."

"Field trip! To another planet! How cool is that? How long does it take?"

"It's a pretty big energy expenditure to open a portal. We try to make every trip worth it," said Benjamin. "We'll probably stay on Sviv about five T-hours. We'll get medical training, and our guardians and the little kids will collect *sva* nuts."

"Five hours," Travis said in a disappointed voice. "I've got maybe an hour and a half, max, before I have to head home. Next time tell me further in advance. Maybe I can arrange some help for Oma and go. Maya, are you going?"

"No. I'm going to meet someone else with a *sissimi* bond."

"Whoa." Travis walked in silence. "Whoa," he said again. "I'd like to see that."

Inside the front door of Janus House, Rowan said, "You lot, gear up and head down to the portal. Benjamin, when are we scheduled to leave?"

"Three fifteen."

Maya checked her watch. Ten minutes to three.

"Get going," said Rowan in his bossiest voice, and the cousins scattered, including Rowan.

Maya and Travis stood alone in the front hall.

A stocky, dark-haired woman in an ochre smock and

blue jeans opened the door to the apartment on the right. Her skin was a warm suede brown, and her face had a lived-in look. Her hair was short and straight. Maya knew she had seen this woman at Saturday Music Night, but she didn't remember her name.

"Maya? Travis?" she said.

"Yes?" Maya said, and Travis said, "Ma'am?"

"Both your teachers are guardians on today's field trip. Did you hear about that?"

"Yes," said Maya.

"I'm Columba Janus. I'm supposed to look after you two this afternoon until Maya's company arrives, which is weird for me. I have an apprentice I'm training, and I work security. They don't generally ask me to entertain. It's not one of my skills." She frowned, then shook her head. "It's going to be a little while until you can meet your visitors, Maya, because the field trip has to use the portal to get to Sviv before your visitors can use it to come here. Travis, you could head home now."

"I don't like to go home before I have to," he said. "Could I meet Maya's visitors, too?"

Columba thought, then said, "I don't see why not, but I'll ask someone who knows more. Come on in."

They followed her into an apartment that was different

from the others Maya had seen in the building. Columba's apartment had big windows that looked out into a forest of potted plants on the verandah. Beyond the plants and the porch railings there was a stretch of the lawn that surrounded Janus House on all sides, and beyond that was Passage Street.

Yellow and white curtains framed the windows. The light coming in was green, filtered by the porch plants' leaves. One of the windows was open a couple of inches.

Columba had a green and black zebra-striped couch, an entertainment unit, a desk with a computer on it, and more plants inside her living room. Some looked rain-forest exotic, with leaves like hands or palm fronds or platters with holes in them, and the flowers looked like insects or butterflies or the heads of dragons. The air smelled like vanilla and cinnamon and hot candle wax.

Through an archway was a kitchen with red counters, wooden cupboards, more windows that faced the porch, and a door that led outside. A pale tan table with two chairs beside it stood in front of one of the windows. Warm daylight gilded the sink and stove.

Maya liked this apartment the best of any she'd been inside in Janus House.

"Have a seat," Columba said, waving toward the green and black couch. Travis and Maya slid out of their backpacks and settled on the couch. Maya got her sketch pad out. The feel of the pencil between her fingers and the smooth paper under the heel of her palm reassured her. She opened to an empty page and sketched Columba's apartment. She got out a second pencil and let Rimi fill in details. Travis leaned back, relaxed almost to sleep, his usual response to any available wait time, and watched the drawing appear.

Columba went to a small round picture on the kitchen wall that showed a flower Maya knew was called a bird of paradise, only it was white instead of orange and blue.

*Is that power picture ugly?* Maya whisper-thought to Rimi. As a design, it matched the house furnishings better than most.

*Not as ugly as most of them,* Rimi thought.

Columba touched the flower and spoke in Kerlinqua.

A familiar voice from the picture answered her. Either Nola Noona or Namdi Sarutha, Maya thought.

Columba cocked her head, then said another phrase. None of the words were ones Maya had learned yet.

Then Columba and whoever was on the other end said, "*Sesstra,*" which Maya did understand: good-bye.

Columba turned to them. "Aunt Noona says you can stay to meet the travelers, Travis, but then Maya and Rimi have to have alone time with them."

"Excellent," said Travis.

"So in the meantime, would you like some tea?"

"Got any water?" Travis asked. "Some without knock-out drugs in it? I would purely appreciate it."

Columba grinned. "I think I can manage that. Maya?"

"Water would be good."

*I wonder if she has anything to eat. You're hungry*, Rimi thought, and Maya's stomach growled. Maya wondered if Rimi had made her stomach do that. What if Rimi could make her burp or fart?

Rimi laughed. *I'm not doing anything except noticing what signals your body sends*, she thought.

Maya burped, startling herself. "Excuse me!"

"Nice one," said Travis.

*You didn't make me do that?* Maya asked Rimi.

*Uh*, thought Rimi.

*Wait! You* did *make me do that?*

*I didn't know I could do anything like that, but when you thought about it, I wondered. So I—well, I—*

Maya felt a burp building again, this time a big one. She

managed to shape the words *all right!* around the burp as it came out.

"Stellar!" said Travis. Columba frowned at Maya.

*Stop that.*

*Okay,* thought Rimi. *I wonder what happens if I—*

*Don't do it!* Maya thought. *At least, not here and now. Don't. Okay?*

*All right,* Rimi thought with a mental sigh. *Ask Columba for food, or I'll go find some for you.*

"Do you have any snacks?" Maya asked quickly. "Please?"

"What did you have in mind?" said Columba.

"Cookies. Crackers. Fruit. Bread. Anything like that."

"Sapphira cooked up a batch of spice bread last night. Wait here and I'll get you a loaf," said Columba. She left the apartment.

"What's with the burps?" Travis asked when the door had closed behind Columba. "That's my department."

"Rimi made me!" Maya said.

"Whoa. Weird. How does that work?"

"I don't know."

*It is gas teased in a particular direction,* Rimi thought.

"Eww!" said Maya.

"What? What did she say?"

Maya told him.

"She can tease gas? Who knew gas had self-esteem problems?" Travis said, and then Columba was back with something the size of a loaf of bread, wrapped in cloth.

"All right," she said. She went to the kitchen, unwrapped the bread, and sliced it on the bread board, then brought out a plate and some cloth napkins. The slices were rich, moist, and dark brown, and they smelled like ginger and cloves and nutmeg.

"Thank you," Maya said as Columba set them on the table in front of her. Now she felt her own hunger.

"You're welcome. I could use a snack myself." Columba grabbed a slice and bit into it. Maya and Travis helped themselves.

"Have you been to Sviv?" Maya asked Columba.

Columba made a face. "It's on my list of least favorite places to visit. That's why I volunteered to host you two today. Much less evil."

"What's a *sva* nut?" asked Travis.

"The only thing that makes Sviv worth going to. They're these nuts as big as your hand. You can slice them like you slice bread, and they're these big, delicious, nutritious, buttery-tasting slices of, well, they're kind of like macadamia nuts in texture and a little in taste. They're like elite travel rations. One nut can keep you alive a week."

"Benjamin said they were going there for medical training," said Maya.

"Yeah, I admit Svivani doctors are good to know when you have medical emergencies."

"How can they doctor people from another planet?"

"Their senses are all geared toward understanding other organisms, how circulatory systems work, muscles, stuff like that. They were champion predators before they civilized themselves. They could always tell the sick prey from the well prey. As a consequence, some of their prey animals evolved into fast, intelligent people, too. They share the planetary government now. So anyway, the Svivani have these extended senses, and they can tell things about plants, too. By now they have huge lists of how plants will act to strengthen or weaken body systems. Some of that they can teach and some they can't."

The power picture chimed. Columba put down her napkin and went to tap it. Noona's voice spoke. After a short conversation, Columba turned to Maya. "Your company has come. They're in the tea room now."

# EIGHT

Maya wrapped an extra piece of spicebread in a napkin and tucked it into her backpack. She stood up, and so did Travis.

"Do you know where the tea room is?" Columba asked.

"Nope," said Maya.

"I'll get you both down there, and I'll get Travis out afterward," Columba said.

"What's the tea room?" Maya had heard of the tea room on the first day of school—a fairy had escaped from it and come to Maya's room in the middle of the night, and that was how Maya got involved with the Janus House people in the first place.

"It's one of the places where we entertain travelers," Columba said. "We have several, with different atmospheres and refreshments, depending on what the travelers need. The tea room is for people who can process Earth air and food."

"Ah," said Maya. They went down the stairs to the tunnels under the apartment complex.

Columba turned down a dark corridor off the main route. Glowing dots of green and blue made spirals and light trails along the walls and ceilings, with an occasional flash of purple or red. At the end of the short spur corridor, Columba paused at a black door with complicated lines of purple, lilac, and lavender inlay. The symbols there looked like some of the symbols Maya had seen in the floor of the portal room, and the writing she'd stared at in the books written in Kerlinqua, which she couldn't read yet.

Columba sang a short phrase of song, repeated it, traced a pattern in the center of the door, and gave it a gentle push. It swung open, letting out soft glowing greenish light and a whoosh of heavy air that smelled like autumn leaves burning.

Sarutha's sister, Noona, stood waiting for them on the other side of the door. "Maya-Rimi, Travis," Noona said, her voice formal. "Please meet Kachik-Vati."

# NINE

Rimi tightened around Maya, an embrace from many overlapping hands.

The tea room had softened corners and a low, round, central table. The dark wood of the tabletop glowed with bits of mother-of-pearl inset in a glittering random scatter. The table stood on a thick carpet patterned in swirls of green, purple, and rose. Around the edges of the room were puffy pillows covered in cloth of the same colors, some large and some small. A door in the left wall was ajar.

Noona stood with her hands clasped in front of her, and beyond her stood someone taller than Maya, taller even than Noona, a person who looked like a stretched pyramid with its base toward the ground and its point toward the ceiling. His skin was the color of bricks, and he had three pale eyes just below the pointed end of the pyramid. He had a lot of arms lying against his body, long, softly furred brown limbs with their hand-ends pointing downward, as though he wore a coat of foxtails. Maya couldn't see if this person had feet. One of his arms was twice as long as the others, and it was a darker color, too, and almost in the center of what might be his chest.

The dark arm rose. At its end was a whorl of tentacles. "Greetings," said the pyramid person from a mouth Maya couldn't see, and the tentacles whirled one way, then the other, then drew their ends together in the center so that they looked like a flower.

"Greetings," Maya said, and gulped. She felt a little dizzy.

"Hiya, big dude," said Travis. Maya glanced at him. He had gone pale, but he was smiling. She hadn't talked to him much about his training to be a *giri*, a human helper to the people who lived in Janus House and their guests, but she guessed some of it must be about encountering people who weren't human. Travis was holding up better this time than he had the first time he encountered otherworlders.

"Greetings to you, smaller dude," said the pyramid person.

Rimi, a faint pressure everywhere against Maya's exposed skin, sent a couple of small jolts into the back of Maya's neck. Maya recognized the calm Rimi could give her when she felt off balance. Her mind steadied; she let her confusion fade and set her brain on memorize so she'd be able to draw pictures of all this later.

"I am Kachik," said the pyramid person, his voice deep and dark. "This is Vati." The darker arm in the center of his—chest?—made a graceful rippling motion. It didn't have elbows; it was many-jointed, like a snake. The tentacles at the end spread into a multi-rayed star, then drew back into a flower shape.

"I'm Maya," Maya said. She swallowed, straightened her shoulders, and reached for the stability Rimi had given her. She gestured toward her friend. "This is Travis. Rimi is—"

Rimi rose up, in shadow form, a stretched version of Maya, translucent, a dark stain in the air, still attached at Maya's feet, but beside her now, a wavery twin.

"Rimi is here," Maya said.

"Oh!" cried Kachik. "Never have I seen such a flower shape!"

The darker arm, Vati, wound around Kachik, then unwound and reached toward Maya and Rimi. Kachik's own arms ended with clusters of tentacles, but there weren't as many tentacles per cluster as Vati had.

"Vati says Rimi is beautiful," Kachik said, "like smoke shaped by wind."

*I told you they would appreciate me, Mayamela,* Rimi thought. She sounded a little shaken.

*Maybe you should compliment them back,* thought Maya. *Tell them Vati looks very useful and has lovely fur.*

Maya repeated this aloud.

"We thank you," said Kachik-Vati. "We greet you. We would know you better if we could. Will you allow it?"

"Travis, it is time for you to leave the tea room," Noona told him.

"Huh?" Travis straightened, took one more look at Kachik-Vati, and then saluted. "Aye-aye, Aunt Sir. Nice to meet you, K-V. Hope to see you later."

"My hope lies there as well," Kachik-Vati said.

Columba opened the door, and Travis went through it. Columba followed him out and closed the door.

Maya looked at Kachik-Vati, then at Noona. "Now what?" she asked.

"Kachik-Vati would like to study you and Rimi. The *sis-simi* bonded have a cache of knowledge they share about how *sissimi* have gone out into the universes, what has become of them. They would collect your bond, and tell you what other bonded have done. Ara-Kita took first news of you to Rimi's home planet. Kachik-Vati is here to take second news of you. In return, Kachik-Vati will help you with *sissimi* issues. They have already given us some help about this."

Maya felt Rimi tense, a vague tightening in the shadow self beside her. Rimi was anxious to find out more about what she was and what she could be, but she and Maya were afraid of having anyone else find out their abilities. "What kind of help did they give you?" Maya asked.

"They have, for instance, told us whom to call should Rimi fall ill," said Noona. "None of us knows how to doctor a sick *sissimi*. She was sick when you first connected to her, wasn't she?"

"Yeah," said Maya. When she had stopped being scared of Rimi, she had worried about her, it was true. Maya had been the cure, though. Easy.

"We have a contact we can call now," Noona said.

"Good."

"Younger two, will you touch selves with me?" Kachik-Vati asked.

"Would that be like it was when Kita and Rimi touched?" said Maya.

"Each *sissimi* is different. Each touch-to-touch, each fusion, is different. It is sharing, though, and it is something we all treasure."

Maya studied Kachik-Vati, who stood quiet, except for Vati's tendrils, which whirled and stopped, whirled and stopped, weaving into different flowery shapes.

*I want to touch them*, Rimi thought. *I want to learn. I want—Vati is my Peter. Well, maybe I'm Vati's Peter and he's my Maya.*

*Is Kachik my Candra?* Maya wondered.

*We can't know until we touch.*

"Okay," Maya said slowly. "Okay. Let's . . . get to know each other." She and Rimi might reveal their secrets. Maybe they'd get new secrets in return.

Two of Kachik-Vati's arms reached for the round table between them. "Noona, your permission to move this?"

Noona inclined her head. "Of course."

Kachik lifted the table and moved it out of the way. All his arms curled against him, the tendrils pointing upward.

Maya straightened up and took three steps toward Kachik-Vati. Rimi moved with her.

Kachik-Vati said, "You look young, as your species looks young. Very young to have established a *sissimi* bond."

"Is there an age limit?" Maya asked.

"Usually *sissimi* bond with people who have spent several years studying for such a gift. There is shared vocabulary that goes across all languages. Some the *sissimi* will know, and some it is the other's job to teach. Only certain people receive the gift of the *sissimi* bond. There are tests one must undergo. You didn't go through them, did you?"

"No," said Maya.

Noona stepped between Maya and Kachik-Vati. "You are to know this child and this *sissimi* bonded out of necessity. The *sissimi* was dying with its original host, and Maya took it over and saved it. She had no training at all."

"Yes," said Kachik. "One of our Lost. We are all grateful the bond succeeded with someone unprepared. Especially since the Lost was too young to leave the vine when it was taken. It is the good kind of chance-meet. All our longing is to help you learn, grow, and be together."

Vati's arm curled and uncurled in an elaborate and graceful dance, its tendrils waving almost hypnotically.

"May we touch now?" Kachik asked.

Maya lifted a hand. "Okay."

Kachik-Vati glided across the floor somehow. Maya still wasn't sure if Kachik had feet. She couldn't even tell if he wore clothes; some kind of skirt hung down to the floor beneath the lowest of his dangling arms, but whether it was part of his skin or an overgarment, Maya didn't know.

Kachik-Vati stopped when they stood two feet from Maya. She looked up into Kachik's eyes. He was two heads taller than she, and his face wasn't very facelike.

"Greetings, small sibling," Kachik said. This close, his voice sounded soft and furry, and seemed to come from somewhere in the middle of him. "I reach to you." Vati curled into a tight spiral, then uncurled, slowly, the tentacles at his tip bunched tight into a spearhead. "Will you reach to me?" Kachik said. Vati paused about five inches from the shadow that was Rimi.

Rimi reached her shadow arm toward Vati's tentacles. As Rimi's edge touched the tips of Vati's tentacles, Maya felt a jolt, a crackling shock that traveled from her chest out to the ends of her fingers and toes. Her hair rustled. The flow Maya had felt when Rimi and Kita touched came again, a caress, a flood of information like light, like heat, the flow going outward and coming in, sipping and sipped. She felt it dimly. Clearer was Rimi's fireworks explosion of joy in the transfer. *Oh, yes, tell me more. Oh! That opens worlds. Oh, that makes more sense than what I thought. Oh! Thank you!*

*Oh!* Rimi's voice vanished into a thrum, joined by another thrum in a different pitch, perfectly harmonizing, both of them ranging up and down but constantly matched. Some of the wonder of the harmonic overtones reached Maya, how the sounds wove into and out of each other, made a song from their mix that belonged to neither voice. Colors stroked parallel tracks across a wide, blank place in Maya's mind, and she reached in with a mental finger to add another shade to the wash of color that wavered back and forth across the endless landscape, a clear yellow that contrasted with their exuberant stripes of green, gray, orange, coral, lilac. She zigged when they zigged and zagged when they zagged, and then their colors bled into hers, and a great humming, jingling, singing warmth swept her up. She heard songs, words, languages, saw images flashing of other places, people, planets.

Her fingertips sizzled. She so wanted paints and paper right now.

She reached out, felt her fingers lace with soft nests of wriggling things, like stroking her fingers through a bunch of warm, spineless snakes. The sensation was pleasant. The snakes wrapped gently around her hands, caging them in building warmth. She knew this was Kachik, that they were embracing now as their *sissimi* embraced. The connection magnified until she was riding a river of memories and information with Rimi, Vati, and Kachik. She couldn't sort it and stopped trying after the initial confusion of the rush. She held on tight to Kachik's tentacles and opened to the flood, trying to capture images to draw.

The song swelled and grew, and the colors spread out and mixed and formed images and shifted again into new shapes and shades.

A flicker of something else broke the flow, which parted around it and rejoined beyond it. Something like a red-tipped thorn. They tried to pause, to study it, but the conversation, the images, the music moved on, and the thorn vanished behind them.

After a short forever, the flow slowed.

*Remember this and this and this,* Vati whispered to Rimi.

*Yes, yes, yes, oh so wide a yes,* Rimi thought, *and thanks thanks love thanks.*

*Release,* thought Vati and Kachik, and Rimi and Maya untwined from the interweave/fusion with them, last touches stroking a promise of connection in the future.

# TEN

Maya took a deep breath and opened her eyes to where she was. She blinked, turned her head.

Noona stood near her, hand resting on Maya's shoulder, but mostly Maya was aware of Kachik, his hand tentacles meshing with her fingers and several of his arms wrapped around her so that she was pressed to his soft, fuzzy, nutmeg-smelling chest, his warmth and the sound of something like hearts beating inside him, a rhythm not human, with bumps bumping into each other, perhaps two things thumping simultaneously, and slightly out of sync with each other. "Are you in good condition, sib?" he asked, his voice a buzz against her cheek and a rumble in the air.

"Mm," she said, blinking. She wasn't sure. "I think."

The dry, snaky embrace of his tentacle-hands loosened, supporting her, but easing her away from him. She swayed, then found her feet. She rubbed her cheek, still warm from being pressed against Kachik's fur.

"Stable?" he asked. "I don't know how, when you only have two points touched down, but it seems to work for many. Have you found the ground, small sib?"

She nodded. "Yes. Thank you. You?"

"My base corners. The ground is solid."

He retracted his arms, releasing her. Rimi and Vati lingered, connected still, and then Vati's arm sagged and Rimi's shadow-self moved back to stand beside Maya. Maya felt the loss of contact.

"There was something," Kachik said. "Did you see it?"

"Yes," said Maya, trying to think of what the thorny thing had looked like. She remembered it as a snag sticking up out of a river of color and music. Or was it a many-tipped spike, like a fork gone mad? It had had a different taste to it, too, like licking a penny. "What was that?"

"A puzzle. A disturbance. Something I have not sensed in any fusion before. Something we must explore, but not just now, I think." He swayed. "This was a lovely fusion, and I need rest."

"Me, too," Maya said.

"Are you all right?" Noona asked Maya. "What happened?"

Maya's mouth tasted like milk and cinnamon. She swallowed and realized she was thirsty and hungry. "A lot," she said. "I'm not sure what." Her stomach growled and her mouth felt like cotton had soaked up all the water in it. *We're hungry* again? she asked Rimi.

*Fusion takes a lot of energy,* Rimi thought. *Kachik-Vati is hungry, too.*

"Nola, could we please get something to eat?" Maya asked Noona.

Noona stroked Maya's back. "Surely," she said. "Kachik-Vati, will you join us for food?"

"I do have need," said Kachik. Vati's arm curled and gestured in a way that looked like *Yes!* to Maya.

Noona took out a communicator, tapped its side, and spoke into it.

"Honored traveler. If you will allow us to restore the table," Noona said.

"A yes yes," said Kachik. He moved the table back into place.

"Maya, please sit," said Noona.

Maya sagged to the floor. She propped her elbows on

the table and cupped her cheeks in her hands.

Noona went to the wall and tapped a pattern on it. A panel opened and she brought out another table, smaller, with telescoping legs. She set it on top of the round table. It came halfway up Kachik-Vati's side. Kachik smoothed two of his tentacle hands over its surface, and then Vati stroked it.

A couple of Janus House cousins came in, carrying trays. One set a tray in front of Maya: a wooden bowl of steaming soup, a mug of hot milk sprinkled with cinnamon, and a cut apple on its own small orange plate. The other cousin set the second tray on the taller table. The tray held a big pottery bowl of something steaming, that was all Maya could tell from below. It smelled a little like wet tennis shoes and damp dog.

Something complicated happened on the side of Kachik that faced her: a fuzzy trunk lifted from the fuzzy surface of his torso and lowered its tip into the bowl. Slurping sounds ensued.

Maya wrinkled her nose and decided she couldn't be too picky about what Kachik-Vati liked to eat, not after how deeply they'd been enmeshed and how well they had worked together. She ate a spoonful of soup and tasted mushrooms, lemongrass, nuts, and the special traveler's spice *palta*, which helped Janus House people adapt to whatever came through the portals. She ate and drank, feeling as though she'd never tasted anything so good before.

"Thanks, Teacher," she said.

"Add my appreciation," Kachik said. "This *cloclo* was prepared correctly, and with just the right amount of *fass*. Delicious."

"You are gracious, Kachik-Vati. Our thanks."

Kachik-Vati straightened, somehow looked taller and more remote. "We have learned many interesting things in the fusion," he said, "some of which I will share with the friendnet, yes, Maya-Rimi?"

"How many are in your friendnet when you go home?" Maya asked.

The skin around Kachik-Vati's eyes crinkled in a smile. "Many many."

"I don't know, Kachik-Vati," Maya said.

Vati sketched a sideways figure eight in the air. "Vati says it is already done," Kachik said. "All know what one knows, sooner or later."

*Do we know everything Vati knows?* Maya thought. *Do we know everything Kita knew?*

*Not everything,* Rimi thought, *but much more than we did before.* A warm golden satisfaction washed through her.

*So much Vati told me about* sissimi. *I have new things to try when we go to the woods.*

*Which I hope will be soon.* Maya checked her watch. "I'm still learning," she said to Kachik-Vati. "I think our friendnet is just you and Ara-Kita."

"Friendnet will be every *sissimi* one you encounter and fuse with, Maya-Rimi," Kachik said.

Maya hugged herself, felt Rimi wrapping around her. "Is every *sissimi* a good person? What if there are others you don't want to friend? What about the two who have been stolen?"

"Rimi was stolen, and is still perfect a one," Kachik said. "*Sissimi* take much from the ones they are partnered with, but there is a core in them that comes from the motherplant and homeplace. They will not be bad."

Maya thought about Rimi sneaking to another room to find out test questions. She liked that Rimi had the power to do this, but she wasn't sure about the ethics of it. It made her so mad when Peter snooped through her stuff—how could she condone snooping? "We have powers," she said slowly to Kachik. "How do you know we'll always use them for good?"

Kachik's eyes crinkled into a smile again. "Probability it will not always happen that way. You must explore. You must try. You must learn and make mistakes. We all do. All the way along this journey, through every portal you go, we meet you. Maybe you go astray some of the time. We all do. We meet you. We meet you now, we meet you later, we hope things go well, we help where we can, and sometimes we can't. We friend you no matter where you are, Maya-Rimi. Know this."

Maya stared up at him, and then she rounded the table and leaned against his front. His smell of Christmas spices, clove, nutmeg, a little peppermint, warmed her. His arms hugged her gently, Vati among them. Rimi stretched and settled inside the embrace as well. Maya felt safe.

Rimi thought in the quiet of Maya's comfort, *How can you know what is good?*

*It's bad if it hurts someone else*, Maya thought.

*You can't tell ahead of time*, Rimi thought. *It doesn't always hurt right away. What if one of the others thinks a thing is good and we think it's bad? What if I think it's good and you think it's bad?*

*I guess . . . we just keep talking about everything and try to figure it out*, Maya thought.

Maya straightened and Kachik-Vati's arms drew away from her, lifting in a pose like the petals of a flower, some kind of salute.

"Good get-together, good get-apart, small sibs," Kachik said.

"You, too," Maya said.

"I will tell the others about your puzzle, small sibs, and someones will come and help you solve it." Kachik's arms danced in a spiral and he moved or levitated back. "Farewell."

"Farewell, big brothers." She waved both hands in mirroring dance moves, and Rimi fluttered like a scarf in the wind.

Maya went back to where her pack rested on the floor. She pulled the straps over her shoulders and shifted to settle the pack on her back.

"Are you rested?" Noona murmured to Kachik-Vati. "Are you fed enough to travel?"

"Both," Kachik said.

"Thank you for the graciousness and gift of your presence," Noona said. She opened another door. It led into the Portal Chamber. Someone Maya didn't know rose from a bench along the wall there and came forward. "These ones are ready to return to their home," Noona told the other woman, who nodded and led Kachik-Vati away.

Noona shut the door, took Maya's hand, and escorted her from the tea room.

# ELEVEN

Noona shut the tea room door carefully and lifted her hands to gesture at the door wards. She sang. The colored spirals and whorls lit up, and the door clicked, lock engaged.

Maya checked her watch. It was four thirty. It felt much later.

They climbed up out of the world under the house and went through the door to the ground floor. Noona shut that door carefully as well, and Maya glanced back at it. A wide door with no knob on the outside.

They went toward the front door. Noona stopped in the hall outside Columba's apartment. She touched Maya's shoulder. "You handled yourself well and made a good connection for us, youngster. It is rare we get a visit from a *mrudim*, and, of course, this is only our second *sissimi* traveler, or third, if we count your Rimi. You do our family proud. Do you want to go home now?"

*How about me? How did I handle myself? How can I, when I don't even have hands?* Rimi wondered. *I do count. I can do that even without fingers.*

*You can have hands whenever you want. And you're wonderful,* Maya thought, and smiled.

*I know. You know. I guess that's enough.*

"Yeah, I guess I'd better head home," Maya said aloud. "Did Travis leave already?"

"I don't know. Columba will know." Noona knocked on Columba's door.

Columba opened the door. "Hey," she said. "How'd it go?"

Noona laid her hand on Maya's shoulder. "A successful meeting, it seemed."

"Maya?" Columba asked.

"Good," Maya said. "They were really nice to us."

"We almost never see *mrudim*. Let alone *sissimi*. You guys got along okay?"

"Yeah," Maya said. She wondered if there was some manual that told you how often various different kinds of people came through the portal. Maybe like a monster manual for D&D.

*We did better than okay*, thought Rimi. *I have a lot of new things to try. Let's go to the woods.*

"Did Travis leave already?" Maya asked Columba.

"Yeah. Travis has left the building." Columba smiled as she said it, as though that was a joke.

"But the other guys are still off on a field trip?"

"Estimated time of return from that one is around midnight," Columba said.

"Jeez," said Maya. "How do they manage to get their homework done and get any sleep when all that's going on?"

"Sometimes they don't," Columba said.

"Huh."

"Sometimes you won't, either, once you start going on field trips. I hope your parents are relaxed about grades."

"I thought all you guys got excellent grades."

Columba frowned. "Yes, in general, the children seem to do well in school." She shrugged. "They work very, very hard."

"On that note," said Maya, "guess I should go do some

of my own homework. Thanks for the hospitality, Columba. Noona, thank you for your help."

"You are welcome, Maya. Harper has been talking to the council about having a series of those with *sissimi* bonds visit and talk to you. We'll let you know when the next one can come."

"Thanks." Maya stopped to dance on the exit mat. The trapped wind in it blew around her, collecting *chikuvny*, the golden dust generated by portal travel, evidence that she had been in contact with someone who had come through the portal.

*I love this,* Rimi said. Maya felt her stretching, dancing with the wind, twining in and out with it. It seemed to partner her, dancing back. In a shimmer of shadow, Maya stamped on the mat. When she'd had enough she stepped off and out through the double front doors.

Travis sat on the porch steps, his social studies textbook open on his knees. He was reading, marking the textbook with pencil taps. He had earbuds in, and his head bobbed to unheard music.

Maya touched his shoulder and he looked up, then smiled at her. He took out the earbuds and tucked them into his shirt pocket with his MP3 player. "How'd it go?"

"He was really nice, and his *sissimi* was—well, I'll know more when Rimi and I get to talk. We're going to the woods now."

"Hah. I was wondering." He stored the book in his backpack and stood up. "Can I come?"

She hesitated, then said, "Yeah."

They walked toward the park together. They couldn't talk to their families about things that happened at Janus House, but they could still talk to each other. They went to different training most of the time, so they liked having time when they could talk about what they were learning. Travis felt like a safe person for Maya to tell about her apprehensions. He even knew she was keeping some secrets about Rimi from Gwenda and Benjamin.

"I've only got twenty minutes," Maya said.

"Me, too."

"Oh, right," she said. "Who's timing?"

"I'll watch the watch," said Travis.

The park was a broad expanse of lawn, marshy now with the fall rains, with stations for Frisbee golf scattered here and there, and many different kinds of trees. Tall chain-link fence caged a set of four tennis courts along one edge, and a basketball court was at the far end. Concrete paths wandered around the edges and across the grass. The woods were toward the side bordered by the creek, a ragged-edged patch of overgrown land with a few trails winding through it and lots of oaks and maples and encroaching blackberry vines and other underbrush. They were very tame woods compared to some Maya had known in Idaho, but they were dense enough. Rimi had figured out how to tighten her shield down to nothing around blackberry canes and snip them off, so she and Maya had made a nest in the heart of a sticker forest, far enough from the path that no one could see or hear them. With Rimi acting as a shield, Maya could push through the blackberry vines to the hideout without a scratch.

Travis had come with them before on days when he and Maya didn't have Janus House training after school. If he crouched and followed right behind Maya, Rimi's shield spread enough to guard him from the vines, too.

When they had settled in the hideout sitting cross-legged and facing each other, Travis said, "So what really happened?"

Maya fished her sketchbook and some colored pencils out of her pack. She opened to a blank page and drew Kachik-Vati. "We fused. Whatever that is."

"Sounds electrical," said Travis. "Or nuclear! Are you really okay?"

"Yeah. Yeah. I guess. I don't really know what happened, except part of it was beautiful, but now Kachik's going to tell a bunch of other people about us. *Sissimi* people, but still."

"Sure. He gets to talk, and we're still stuck with silence."

Rimi darkened her shadow form and walked around the clearing, snipping vines that had poked in since the last time she and Maya had been here. She looked like an independent entity, except for a line of shadow that stretched from her left foot to Maya's left foot. If Maya narrowed her eyes and peered through her lashes, Rimi almost looked solid.

"Rimi, what did you learn?" Maya asked.

*One thing was how Vati hooks to Kachik*, Rimi said. She sat in front of Maya and stretched out a shadow arm to the center of Maya's chest. *He says this is a way many* sissimi *bonds behave.* Her shadow self drew tighter in on itself, losing its human shape, until it was a dense tube of darkness about two feet long. Maya felt pressure against her chest, then varying touches, as though fingertips pressed against her, and then a flurry of stabs that shocked more than hurt her.

Rimi turned solid.

A new limb had sprouted from Maya's chest, a snaky

limb like Vati had been, only with a hand on the end instead of a cluster of tentacles. Its skin was the color of Maya's skin.

The limb rose, moved itself in a jerky circle, and Maya *felt* it, as though her nerves extended along this limb. She clenched her eyes shut, then opened them, and tried to move the new arm. It jiggled. She felt that, too. *Bend*, she thought, and the arm bent. It bent in crazy directions an arm shouldn't go, but it didn't hurt, and she could almost control it. She felt the little bones and muscles working together, a strange, sinuous rippling. *Wow, Rimi!*

*I've been thinking about how human bodies work. There are better ways*, Rimi thought. *This way is good for manipulation, but not for strength, maybe. I'll have to test different things.*

*Can it attach anywhere on me?* Maya looked down at her three arms. She turned her original arms so that her palms were up, then down. She touched the new arm with her right hand—smooth skin, warm. The central arm moved under her touch. She felt a shifting of hard bits under a padding of skin and muscle.

Rimi thought, then said, *For you to be able to use it, there has to be a confluence of*—the hand wavered, trying to finish a thought Rimi didn't have words for. *If it's just me using it, I guess I could—I don't even know if it would have to be attached, as long as some of me is attached to you somehow. But that—*

Maya thought the hand into a fist and it responded. *Wow, Rimi. This is us being together in a whole new way.*

*I like it,* Rimi thought. *See what you can do with us.*

The hand picked up one of her pencils and sketched another arm onto Kachik's pictured body. The control of the pencil was crude to begin with, but as Maya worked at it, it got better.

"That is just *so* wrong," Travis said.

*Now me,* Rimi said, and the hand was no longer in Maya's control. It picked up three pencils at once, sprouted extra fingers—such a strange, pushing sensation, as though she were a plant under the earth shoving out roots and shoots—and shaded in Kachik's surface, making tiny strokes that showed his fur.

"Even wronger!" Travis said.

The new hand dropped the pencils and rose. The many fingers wiggled a wave at Travis. He flinched, then settled. "Hi, Rimi," he said. "Is that all you now?"

The hand waved up and down, like a nod.

"Freaky, dudette. You don't want to go out in public like that."

The hand shook side to side, a negative.

"Well, all right. As long as you know. You're making Maya into an alien."

*Yes, I am,* Rimi thought. The hand snaked around and patted Maya's cheek. *Well, enough of that.* Rimi let the arm and hand unspin itself back to shadow.

Maya pulled out her T-shirt front and studied the new oval hole in it. She poked a finger through. "Huh."

*Oops,* thought Rimi. *Gotta watch that. Sorry.*

"Doesn't matter," Maya said. "Only where did it go?"

*I probably made it into part of me,* Rimi thought.

Travis looked at his watch. "Yikes! Rise and run, kids!"

Rimi expanded her shield bubble to include Travis as they pushed out of the thicket in a different direction from the way they had come in. Before, she had made Maya into a shield Travis could hide behind. This time she stretched far enough around him that he could walk upright through the thorny blackberry canes instead of crouching. "Way to go, Sis-sis," he said. "Way cool. Liking the new skills."


"Hey," Peter said when Maya ran into the kitchen just in time for the five P.M. curfew, "I want to talk to you."

"Have to set the table," Maya said. "Hi, Mom." Her mother was chopping lettuce for a salad and frying corned beef hash on the stove; the kitchen smelled good. Her father sat at the table, buttering bread and sprinkling garlic powder on it.

Maya shrugged out of her backpack. She washed her hands, grabbed a rag, and wiped off the dining room table, then set out the sunflower place mats. Peter followed her around the table.

"This morning your shadow waved at me," he muttered when Maya reached the far end of the table from the kitchen.

"Sure," said Maya. "Wanna see it happen again?" She turned on the overhead light and waved at Peter, and her shadow waved, too.

"Come on. You know what I'm talking about. It wasn't like that."

Maya turned away from him. She collected napkins and silverware from the sideboard and walked around the table, laying out places.

"Maya," Peter said from right behind her.

She jumped and knocked a fork off the table.

Rimi caught it.

# TWELVE

Maya and Peter stared at the fork floating in the air. Then Maya grabbed it and put it back on the napkin where it belonged.

"Don't pretend that didn't happen," Peter said.

"I can't talk to you about this."

"Sure you can. It has something to do with all the time you're spending with those people next door, right? Right?"

"What does?" asked Candra, breezing in. "Peter, are you getting the dirt? Maya, you're such a danged clamshell about Janus House. Sure, I saw Gwenda's closet, but that didn't tell me much. It just made me more curious! What's up with Benjamin? What do you know about Fiona? What about that crazy old lady who's always watching us from the porch?"

"Namdi Sarutha's not crazy," Maya said.

"Hah! You *can* talk about them! Spill!"

"Why don't you ask your own questions? That guy Evren seemed interested in you yesterday. He might be able to tell you something."

"I tried calling over there. Do you know there's like, only one phone number listed for a Janus? How many Januses live in that pile? How can they all share one phone? The woman who answered wouldn't even take a message for Evren. 'You don't find Evren, he finds you,' she told me. What's up with that?"

"I don't know," Maya said. "I guess he's around a lot, but I never saw him before yesterday."

"Don't you think that's peculiar?" Candra asked.

"No. I see some people over there a lot, and there are bunches of them I never run into."

Candra pondered, then said, "You thought Evren liked me? I thought he did, too."

"Sure seemed like it," Maya said. "Even though you were snoopy and rude."

"I was not either rude to him."

"You attacked him with questions."

"That's what I do to everyone," said Candra.

"Well, anyway, he seemed like he wanted to get to know you better."

"Exactly. That's the message I got, too. So I'm trying to see him, but I apparently don't have the clout to get hold of him. You're all I've got until I make contact with him again. So give. Do they have their own religion? Is that why they won't help me travel? They only help people who belong to their religion?"

"I can't tell you, Candra," Maya said. "No matter how many times you ask, my answer will be the same."

"You make me so mad!" Candra said, and showed her clenched teeth.

"Like that's hard to do," said Maya.

Peter tugged on her sleeve. "Maya," he said, his head coming forward, chin first, like a turtle about to chomp some lettuce.

"Yes, all right, let me finish and then we can go to your room." She got glasses and plates from the kitchen and set them on the table.

"What are you going to do in Peter's room, huh?" Candra asked.

"Nothing," said Maya.

"Nothing," said Peter. They stuck their tongues out at their older sister and raced for the stairs.

"Mo-om!" Candra cried behind them.

They dashed into Peter's room and shut the door.

Maya hadn't been in Peter's room since moving day, when she had helped carry any boxes anyone handed her off the back of the moving van. The boxes had all been labeled. She had brought several to Peter's room. It used to be a clean, bare place with nice windows looking toward the street.

Now it smelled like wood shavings and animal pee and rotting orange peels.

Peter had two cages set up on his desk under the windows. Blond hooded rats lived in one of them, and a couple of guinea pigs, one short-haired calico and one long-haired beige, lived in the other. The guinea pigs meeped. Peter went over to their cage and dropped a few cherry tomatoes in, and they squealed in delight and settled down to munch.

The pet cages were fairly clean—much cleaner than the rest of the room.

Peter had piles of comic books stacked around the room, and he hadn't made his bed in who knew how long.

Dirty clothes lay in twisted tangles on the floor and draped over the desk, the dresser, and the chair. Plates with dried-up food and not-dry-enough orange peels on them lurked under the desk and on the bedside table.

"Gah, Peter, you're worse than I am," Maya said.

Peter leaned his back against the closed door to the hallway and surveyed his room. "Yuck," he said. "I guess I haven't been paying attention." He grabbed a laundry bag from the floor of his closet and stuffed clothes in it. "Have a seat," he said when he had cleared off the desk chair.

"Thanks." Maya settled on the chair and studied the rats.

*What are those?* Rimi asked. She sent out exploratory arms toward the cages on the desk.

*You haven't met the pets yet?* Maya wondered.

*Somehow I didn't explore here while you were asleep. Something in the overall aura turned me away. I know what's in Candra's jewelry box and what's in the bottom drawer of her dresser. I know where your mother keeps a secret stash of chocolates, and I know what's hidden inside your father's hat on the top shelf of the closet, but I never came in here before.*

*What's hidden inside Dad's hat?*

*Is it okay for me to tell you that? I don't understand when I can tell you things and when I shouldn't.*

*I know, I've been very confusing about this. I guess I don't need to know right now.*

The rats congregated near the cage wall closest to Maya. She saw their fur moving. *What are you doing?* she asked.

*They are soft, and they like this. I lizzer it. It makes a glow. What is a pet?*

*Animals we take care of and own.*

Rimi twanged a couple of the bars on the cages. *Pets live in enclosures they can't get out of when they want to,* she said.

*That's part of little pets. I guess it's part of Sully's thing, too. He can go in the backyard and anywhere in the house, but he can't just run around loose. If we want to walk him, we put him on a leash.*

*Sully has an always curfew.*

*Huh. A curfew is like being a pet?* A curfew kept Maya from running around loose anytime she wanted to, but she didn't think it made her a pet. For one thing, she could disobey the curfew. Then she'd have to live with the consequences. She could still do it.

Sully got out sometimes. He was still a pet.

*Am I a pet?* Rimi thought.

*No!* Maya thought. Then she remembered stroking the egg-seed Rimi had been before she hatched, loving the way it purred. Rimi had seemed like her little pet then. That was before Rimi spoke to Maya, before she had a name. *You're not a pet*, Maya thought slowly, *but I don't think everyone knows that.* She remembered Noona talking to Maya as though Maya was the only person who had met Kachik-Vati. Maybe people had trouble knowing Rimi was a person because they couldn't see her.

"So are you going to tell me about the fork now?" Peter said. He had straightened the covers on his bed and was sitting on top of them.

"I—" Maya felt the familiar paralysis in her tongue and throat. "I can't."

"Why not?"

"I can't. I physically can't."

Peter frowned. "I don't understand."

"And I can't explain it—"

*But Harper didn't put a silence on me*, Rimi thought. *Plus, I want to explore your silence and see if I can relax it.* Maya felt warmth in her throat and mouth. *Try to say it again.*

Before Maya could open her mouth, Peter spoke. "Do you have a poltergeist?"

"I don't—huh?"

"You know, the kind of ghost teenagers get that makes noises and throws things." Peter lifted a fat, tattered, blue-green book off his bedside table and flashed it at her:

*Paranormal Phenomena.* "I've been studying and that seems like the closest thing I can figure to what you do."

Peter had been reading up on her and Rimi? She had had no idea. How many times had they slipped? She had thought she was doing a good job of disguising her changes, but maybe Rimi had been doing other things when Maya wasn't watching. "Huh. Maybe I do."

"Like, it happens to disturbed teenagers, and you're pretty disturbed."

"What do you mean by that?"

"Because of Steph," Peter said. He stared down at the book on his lap and bit his lower lip.

"Oh." So many things had happened lately that Maya hadn't had much time to think about her best friend. She felt guilty. Stephanie was dead, but a way to keep her alive was to visit her in memory. *If I don't think about her, does she die all over again?* Maya wondered, not for the first time.

"Can you control it?" Peter asked.

"No." Not unless Rimi wanted to do what Maya suggested. Rimi was pretty agreeable on most things, but Maya didn't even want to try ordering her around.

"But you know what I'm talking about. You're not going to deny it."

Rimi had switched to petting the guinea pigs, and they made contented burbling sounds.

Maya stopped watching the fur ripple across the guinea pigs' backs and looked at her younger brother. She shook her head.

"I wish *I* had a poltergeist," Peter said. "It would be so cool. Things moving around without anybody lifting them. When kids have poltergeists, sometimes stones fall on the roof of their house, mysterious rocks. Geologists can look at them and tell they're not from around there. It's like they come from space. And there are knocks on the walls or under the tables, and—are you sure you can't make it do things like that?"

"I can't make it do anything," Maya said.

Rimi opened and closed a drawer in Peter's dresser.

"Whoa! Whoa! What was that?" Delighted, Peter jumped up and ran to the dresser.

Rimi picked up all the dirty dishes in the room and piled them by the door. Peter was staring at the dresser and missed the new phenomenon until the dishes clattered as they settled in a stack. "Whoa!" Peter turned around and stared.

Every dirty piece of clothing draped around the room

rose and stuffed itself into the laundry bag. "Whoa!" Peter grabbed the laundry bag out of the air and peered inside.

He looked at Maya. "Usually, poltergeists mess things up and break them. How'd you score one who does housekeeping?"

"Just lucky, I guess."

"Hey, poltergeist!" Peter said. "Thanks for helping. Do you clean animal cages?"

Rimi picked up the calico guinea pig, opened the cage door, and brought it out. It shrieked stridently, then settled into contented muttering as Rimi stroked and cradled it. She brought it to Maya and set it in her lap.

"Wow," Peter whispered.

"She doesn't take orders," Maya said. "She does what she likes."

"It's a girl? Poltergeists are girls and boys?"

"You know more than I do," Maya said. She pointed to the book he'd left on the bed.

"Not about *your* poltergeist," Peter said. He took his laundry bag to the bed, shoved the book over to make room, and settled down.

"That's true. She's not really a poltergeist, Peter, but I can't tell you what she is."

"Don't you know?"

"Uh-huh, but I can't talk about it."

"You said that before."

"There's a—" She felt the silence lock her throat again. She stroked her throat with her hand, trying to ease the closing. Rimi flowed into her mouth, a warmth in her throat. *Words! Words lock up words! There are little* squizzles *in the walls of your air tube. I* flurr *them, spinning green brown things in here that close your throat. I will unspin them!*

Maya spread her hand against the skin of her throat. Surges of warmth and coolness alternated. She felt like she had a fighting fur ball stuck in her throat, and she coughed and almost choked, but then it smoothed out and she could breathe again.

"Are you all right?" Peter asked, peering at her.

"I-I-I hope so. Rimi?"

*Say something you're not supposed to.*

"Janus House is magic," Maya whispered. Nothing stopped her. She swallowed, her hand on her throat. *Rimi. Rimi. Thank you.* Maya dropped her hands to cuddle the guinea pig in her lap. Its furry warmth comforted her.

"Sure, I knew that," said Peter.

"You did?"

"Yeah. That's one of the reasons I checked these books out of the library. I've been watching Bran at school and all those Janus House people during Music Night. Bran is so quiet. But sometimes he does weird stuff when he thinks no one's watching. He won't really look me in the face, though. I try talking to him to see if we can be friends, and he looks at the ground and kind of shifts away." Peter pounded the bed with a fist. "It's so frustrating having someone not be there when they're right there, you know? I don't know how to get past that."

*Fairy dust,* Maya thought. Chikuvny. *A disguise, so they think you're one of them.*

Peter continued, "Sometimes when those guys sing on Music Night, strange things happen. Lights shine where there aren't any lights, and the air tastes funny. I snuck my camera down one night to try to get pictures of it, but nothing happened that night. Next week, the lights went crazy, but I forgot to bring my camera. I can't paint pictures of it the way you can.

"That's why I want to see *all* your art," he added. "You're painting stuff that happens next door, aren't you?"

# THIRTEEN

Maya drew a deep breath. The true test of Rimi's relaxing of Harper's commands came now. "Yeah," she said. "Yeah." She touched her throat again.

"The aliens with wings and funny hair, the people dancing around that colored fire, the alien egg?"

Maya nodded.

"The dead boy," Peter said slowly.

Maya swallowed, felt Rimi's rush of sadness at Bikos's loss again. She nodded.

Peter's lips tightened. "Since then, you've been using up a lot of sketchbooks, but most of them aren't here. Sometimes I find one in your backpack and it's full of amazing pictures.

Then it's gone and there's a new one. What happens to them when they're full?"

"Peter, how many times do I have to tell you not to snoop through my stuff?" Maya asked, angry with him all over again. She had to stop leaving her backpack any place but in her room. She wondered if Gwenda could help her ward her room or her pack or both against Peter.

"I know you hate it, but it seems like the only way to find out what's going on, Maya, and I want to know. I mean, you're hanging out in a house full of magic users, and you draw pictures of big scary centipedes and monsters. What if something bad happens to you? I want to at least have a clue."

"If I tell you what's going on, would you quit going through my stuff?"

He clenched his hands into fists. "I don't know. Maybe. I have this hunger. You know. Candra has it, too, but she does something else with it."

*I can help you guard things from him*, Rimi thought.

*You can? And you waited this long to tell me?*

*But I want Peter to be part of us. I want him for my brother, too.*

Maya sighed. Her anger ebbed. "I guess if I were you and

you were me, I'd want to know what was going on, too."

He smiled, relieved.

"And my new friend the poltergeist wants you to know."

"What you have is not really a poltergeist," Peter said.

"No."

"Is it Stephanie's ghost?"

"No. I wish, but no." She stroked the guinea pig. "Peter, you have to swear you won't tell anybody about this, okay?"

He looked up at her. "Okay," he said. "I do so swear."

"On all the things you hold sacred."

"On all the things I hold sacred."

"Cross your heart and hope to die, stick a needle in your eye?"

He made a cross over his heart and swore.

"It's my new best friend, Rimi. She's invisible most of the time."

"Is she a ghost?"

"No. She's an alien."

Peter frowned. "I don't get how aliens fit in with magic. What do you mean?"

"It's confusing." Maya stood up and set the guinea pig back in its cage.

"You got that right."

"I don't understand it either, but it all mixes up. Rimi is my new best friend. She's like a part of me, like a shadow, but she's her own self and makes her own decisions. She's wanted to talk to you for a while."

"She can talk?"

"Uh—well, she can talk to me, anyway. I don't know if she can speak out loud."

"Rimi?" Peter said. "Are you here? Knock once for yes and twice for no. That's how they talk to spirits at séances sometimes. I don't know if it works with poltergeists."

Rimi knocked three times on the wall by Peter's bed.

"Three times? Three times means what?" Peter flipped through the book, checked the index at the back, then looked up with a frown. "You're teasing me."

Rimi knocked once.

Peter frowned, then smiled. "Oh, okay. So, about the housekeeping thing—"

Rimi upended the laundry bag and scattered dirty clothes all over.

"Yikes," said Peter.

"Okay, you know that's not me doing it, right?" Maya asked.

"Yeah, I get that."

Two grass-stained T-shirts danced in the air, moving together and apart, mirroring each other's moves. "Wow," Peter whispered. "Wow, Rimi. Wow, wow, wow."

"Do poltergeists do things like that?" Maya asked.

"I don't think they usually know how to dance," said Peter.

Pounding sounded at the door. The T-shirts dropped to the ground. "Hey, talk louder so I can hear you," Candra yelled. "What are you twerps up to in there?"

"None of your beeswax," Maya yelled back.

"You can run, but you can't hide!" Candra yelled.

"That doesn't even make sense," cried Maya. "We're not running. We're not even hiding. You know where we are!"

"Yeah, yeah," Candra said. She stomped away.

Maya and Peter giggled.

"Is she gone?" Maya whispered.

Peter frowned.

Rimi eased part of herself under the door. *No. She snuck back. She has a glass to her ear and it's against the door. What is that?*

*That helps you hear through walls*, Maya thought. She whispered to Peter, "Rimi says Candra's still listening to us."

He whispered back, "How can she tell?"

"Rimi is good that way. She can sneak under doors and check stuff out."

"That is just *so cool*. You are the luckiest person on Earth," he whispered.

Rimi ruffled his hair. "Hey," he said out loud, startled.

"She really likes you," Maya whispered.

"Hey," he said, softer, and smiled. "I like you, too, Rimi." He slid off the bed, tiptoed to the door, and yanked it open. Candra fell into the room, tucked and rolled so the water glass in her hand didn't shatter.

"Wow." Candra rose to her feet as though she had never fallen. "You sure haven't been keeping up with the cleaning, little brother."

"Yeah, yeah," said Peter. "Tell me something I don't already know."

Maya had a sudden swooping fear that Candra had heard everything. She tried to backtrack, wondering what words they had said aloud. Alien. Magic. She knew she had said both of those words.

"So. You were talking about poltergeists . . ." Candra let her voice trail off, waiting for someone to fill in a blank. Maya had seen Candra use that trick before.

Oh, good, Maya thought. Candra had fixed on poltergeists, the least worrisome of the words. Maybe she hadn't heard everything.

"Yeah, poltergeists," said Peter. He waved the paranormal book at Candra. "Do you have one? You're disturbed enough."

"I don't have a poltergeist! But Maya has one, right?"

"No," Maya and Peter said together.

"Oh, like I'm going to believe you now! You drive me crazy!"

"I don't have a poltergeist," Maya said. "I swear."

"So is it something else? You have something else?"

Maya stood and brushed past Candra. "See you later, Peter. I better check with Mom and see if I finished my chores."

"Hey," Candra said, but she let Maya go by.

# FOURTEEN

Tuesday at lunch, Travis sat at the Janus House table. "How was the field trip?" he asked.

Twyla and Kallie groaned.

"Sviv *so* sucks!" Twyla said.

Kallie coughed theatrically. "My throat's still sore, and I think I'm getting a rash." She showed the backs of her hands. They were red and had small bumps on them.

"You know you're not supposed to touch any of the plants," Rowan said.

"But those flowers looked so soft."

Gwenda took a wrapped parcel out of her lunch tin. "The Littles collected some good *sva* nuts, anyway," she said, and opened the waxed paper to reveal something the size of a grapefruit but pale and solid-looking. She tapped it. It fell apart in slices. She handed them around to everyone.

Maya held hers in front of her. It was like a round piece of wood, about a quarter of an inch thick, only the edges felt softer and there weren't any splintery parts. Rimi explored it. *Food*, she said. *Safe. Good for you, even.*

Maya took a bite. Not really a crunchy texture; solid but soft. Buttery, nutty, a little salty, with faint undertones of garlic and smoke. "Yum," she said. She looked up. Everyone else had already eaten their slices.

Gwenda laughed and passed around the rest of the slices.

"Did you learn anything good?" Maya asked.

"Some new healing songs," Benjamin said. "Except they don't use songs, really, they do something else with sound and pictures, and we have to transpose it to make it work for us. That's the hard part, the transposing. Aunt Sarutha is really good at it. I'd like to learn how to do that. How did your *sissimi* meeting go?"

"Good," said Maya.

"Do you know what species the partner was?" said Gwenda.

"I don't. Aunt Noona said what he was, but I don't

remember. He was like a big furry pyramid with lots of arms, no feet, and three eyes, and his *sissimi* was one of his arms. He smelled good, but his food stank. He had a trunk like an elephant, only furrier."

"Sounds like a *mrudim*," Benjamin muttered. "We hardly ever see those. Most of them don't like to portal."

"*Mrudim* sounds right," said Maya. "His name was Kachik."

"He had a sense of humor," Travis said. "And a real A-plus voice. Kind of like if a bear could talk."

"You met him, too?" Rowan asked.

"Yeah, sure, why not? Didn't have training to go to, since my teacher was off with you guys, so I tagged along to the tea room."

"Harper said that was okay?" asked Rowan.

"Noona did, anyway." Travis shrugged. "What's your problem, Rowan?"

Rowan stared at Travis, sparks kindling in his amber eye. Then he shook his head and looked away. "Still trying to adjust to the new open," he muttered. "Sorry."

"They chased me out before Maya got too involved with the guy, anyway."

"What does that mean, too involved?" asked Benjamin. He leaned forward.

"We did this *sissimi* thing called fusion," Maya said. "I think we did it with Ara-Kita, too, only that time, it was more Rimi and Kita. I was sort of nearby but not really involved."

"Fusion," Benjamin said. "Sounds intense."

"Yes."

"Is that something you've done pictures of?"

"Not yet," said Maya. She frowned. "There were a lot of colors and things—it's in my head, but it's not in my mind, so I don't think it can come out of my hand yet."

*I wonder if I could draw it,* Rimi thought.

*Let's try that! Maybe after school? Would you want to make an arm to do it, or would you just do like you do when you're using my pencils and I can't see you?*

*Don't know,* Rimi thought. *Wait till we have private time and try them both, maybe.*

"Hey," Travis said. "I have a favor to ask."

Gwenda set down her spoon and tin cup of soup. "What is it?"

"Would some of you come to my house after school today? The caretaker needs to leave early, so I have to go straight home. I'd like to introduce some of you to my oma. I can't talk to her about anything in Janus House, since Harper junked my tongue. But maybe you guys could tell her what happened, about me being a *giri* in training and all that." He glanced at Rowan. "That should be okay, right?"

Rowan nodded. "Since she's *giri* herself."

The Janus House kids looked at each other.

"I can come," Gwenda said, "if one of you will say I'll be late for singing class today."

"Me, too," said Benjamin.

"Do you need me as well?" Rowan asked. "At the business meeting last week, we discussed your oma. Aunt Noona said we should send help to her, since she had been our help for so long. We should talk to her about what she needs and what we can give."

"Why don't I just introduce her to Gwenda, Benjamin, and Maya—if you can come, Maya—and we can talk about the other stuff later?"

"All right," said Rowan.

"I can come," Maya said. "I'd like to meet her." Tuesday afternoons she didn't have training at Janus House, and she hadn't found an after-school art class to sign up for yet. She was curious about Travis's oma. He spoke of her with such tenderness, and then sometimes he was harassed and irritated about having to take care of her. She already had several pictures of Oma in mind. A real image would be better than invented ones.

"So, good," Travis said. "Meet you guys out front after last period." He went back to sucking Jell-O worms out of a cube of red cafeteria Jell-O with a straw.

After school, Gwenda, Maya, and Benjamin fell into step beside Travis. Leaf smoke scented the air. The sky was brilliant blue, and the fall leaves glowed orange and yellow on the trees along Passage Street. The trunks of the trees looked black and skeletal.

Travis glanced toward Dreams & Bones as they passed. Lots of people were inside, looking around.

"Do you go in there?" Maya asked Travis.

*I want to go inside*, Rimi thought. *There's something—a skrill—something. I want to* sisti *it.*

"When I have time," Travis said. "Weyland has a lot of great stuff, and he knows everything he's got. He's like a talking comics encyclopedia."

"Wait. Wait. There's a store here? How long has it been there?" Benjamin asked. "I never noticed it before." His voice had an edge to it.

"Nor have I," said Gwenda. She gripped Maya's arm and stopped to stare toward the store. "The windows are cloudy. What's inside?"

Maya looked into the café. The light was bright but touched with gold, making it look warm inside. Kids and grown-ups were sitting at the tables, reading comic books or working on their laptops or iPhones, drinks in tall, colored, flared cups beside them, plates of pastry next to their computers. Past the café part of the store were the wooden shelves full of books, manga, comics, and anime-related toys. There were lots of kids in the store, some of them talking to the proprietor, who leaned back against the glass case containing dice, role-playing game cards, and other game equipment.

"You can't see inside?" Maya asked Gwenda. *Rimi, do you see the store?*

*I do. It looks like a store full of people, but—there's something—I remember—something familiar about this place. An energy trace. A taste from before I could taste.*

Gwenda said, "I see soapy windows and a locked door. It looks run-down and vacant."

"It's a store," Benjamin said. "I can tell that much." He narrowed his eyes and stared at the sign. "There's writing on the sign, but it's faded, and some of the letters are missing."

"You guys are kidding, right?" Travis said. "Dreams and Bones has been here about a year and a half. All new." He pointed to the sign, which to Maya looked sparkling and clean, red letters outlined in yellow against a dark brown background: DREAMS & BONES.

Benjamin shook his head. "That's not what I see."

"I don't even see a sign," Gwenda said. She touched some of the charms on her bracelet and sang softly in Kerlinqua. Her eyes widened. "Oh! Oh! Benjamin!"

He sang the same phrase she had, and staggered back, almost stepping off the curb. "Oh! I've never seen wards like this before. We have to tell Columba."

"But—" Travis said.

"It'll keep," said Gwenda. "It's already kept a year and a half. Probably it's not an immediate threat. And we promised Travis we'd go home with him today."

Benjamin sucked on his lower lip. "Okay," he said.

They turned away from Passage Street and headed north. Some porches of the houses they passed bore pumpkins, and one yard had a witch scarecrow and her arched-back black cat lurking near a big cauldron on the front lawn. Another house had fake spiderwebs with big black spiders hanging from the porch eaves. Someone else had put up tombstones on their front lawn, and another yard sported leaf bags that looked like giant skulls staring toward the street.

"Are you going to dress up for Halloween?" Maya asked Travis.

"Probably not so much," he said. "I'll be handing out candy with Oma, most likely. Me and the digital camera. We like to have pictures of the best costumes. This way." He turned from Passage Street onto Thirty-fourth.

The houses got bigger as they walked, the yards more expansive, more hidden behind various kinds of hedges. The decorations here were smaller and less fun, more like things picked by grown-ups who didn't know any kids.

"Interesting neighborhood," said Benjamin.

"Yeah. You never see anybody playing outside at these houses," Travis said.

"When you were little, did you play in the yard?" Maya asked.

"I played all over my old neighborhood. Dad and I have only lived with Oma since the crash."

"When was the crash?"

"A year ago."

"Great-aunt Elia died about a year and a half ago," said Benjamin, "and I guess your oma didn't connect much to anyone else at Janus House. Great-uncle Harper must have known her—Elia was his favorite sister and they spent a lot of time together—but he didn't sponsor her to come back after Elia died. I don't know what that's about. There are two other *giri* at Janus House now. One of them, Miss Delia, was chosen by Cousin Columba, and she's friends with several other people now, and does errands for all of them. She's about sixty. The other one, Morgan Fetters, is *really* old, and was recruited by Istar Jerusalah, the one who used to be in charge of everything before Harper took over. He's too old to do much for us. Some of the cousins stop by and check on him and take him places if he needs help."

"Uh . . . was I supposed to get chosen by somebody?" Travis asked. "If I was, who is it?"

Benjamin laughed. "That's right," he said. "Somebody has to pick you! I'll do it."

"Does that mean we're best friends?"

Benjamin looked sideways at Travis, still grinning. "Works for me."

"Okay," said Travis. "Maybe we should, you know, like, get to know each other better. What would happen if you sat with my other buddies at lunch sometime, instead of at the Janus House table? Would the universe implode?"

"I don't know," said Benjamin. "Let's try it and see."

"Benjamin, we're not supposed to—" Gwenda said.

"It's different if the person is *giri*," Benjamin said.

They walked in silence for a little while, and then Gwenda said, "Maybe I can get a *giri*, too."

"Or you could go sit at a different table with me

and Rimi," Maya said. "What do you think about Helen Halloran?"

"She's always nice," Gwenda said. "Nicer than most. You know? We have a rep at school. Most people just ignore us. Helen has lots of friends, but she still says hi to us once in a while."

"What about Sibyl Katsaros?"

Gwenda frowned.

"There's something off about her," Travis said.

"Yes," Gwenda said. "She has music on her, only some of the pitches are tuned differently. There's something. . . . Something."

"So it's not just me," Maya said.

"She noticed Rimi," Benjamin said. "Usually if people see something strange, like pencils moving by themselves, their brains make up some kind of excuse for it, and they forget it. She watched. I think she saw."

"We're here," Travis said. He stopped at a house with a low rock wall in front of it. Some of the rocks were huge chunks of agate, and some were black-and-white streaked granite, with gleaming mica. The wall was just the right height and width to sit on comfortably, and between it and the sidewalk was a little strip of garden that hosted a lot of bushy chrysanthemums, most blooming in colors of rust and fire. An opening in the middle of the wall gave onto a flagstone pathway that ran between flanks of overgrown garden to the front porch of the house. Two steps led to the front porch with a wheelchair ramp beside them.

A cardboard skeleton was tacked to the door. It was smiling.

Travis crossed the porch, unlocked the front door, and stood back, revealing a wide hallway with dark walls. Framed art hung against the dark paneling. A runner carpet with a pattern of autumn leaves led toward the far end of the hall. Light came from the doorway to a room on the right side.

"Oma? Artemis? I'm home," Travis called as he followed the others into the hall.

"Well, thank goodness, that," said a woman who came out of the room with light leaking from it. She was skinny and had brown, bushy hair and sandy brown skin. She pulled a beige jacket on over her orange dress, grabbed a messenger bag, and slung it over her shoulder. "You tend to her right now. She needs to go to the bathroom." The woman rushed past them and out the front door.

Travis slid out of his pack and ran to the room. "Oma?"

"Yes, dear," said a strong voice. "If you could—Artemis didn't even want to start, and we were waiting—"

"Sure."

Maya stood in the hallway with Benjamin and Gwenda. She thought it would be better to wait until Travis and his grandmother had sorted themselves out. Rimi wasn't so patient. She sent out a snaky arm and peeked around the corner, just as Travis said, "I brought company home, Oma."

"Oh, dear. Oh, dear."

"We'll be a little while, guys," Travis called.

"Sure," Benjamin said. "We'll wait out here till you're ready."

Maya studied the artwork on the walls, and so did Gwenda and Benjamin. Several pencil sketches of people in the midst of farm activities, with strong strokes that gave a sense of large, muscular people working hard with wheat and grain and cattle. Two watercolor landscapes, the colors more vivid than watercolors usually were—a lake below steep, snow-topped mountains, and a beach during a storm.

"Do you like them?" Gwenda murmured under cover of wheelchair noises, a door shutting gently, and soft shuffles and murmurs from the room ahead.

"Yes," said Maya. "This one especially." Spare outlines

sketched a barefoot boy in white shirt and pants with suspenders, his hand on the headstall of an ox taller than he was.

Or was it an ox? Did it have three horns?

Returning, Rimi brushed her cheek.

*What did you find?* Maya thought, *or do I even want to know?*

*The old one has many different kinds of pain. She is sad like my other Other just before he died.*

Maya hugged herself. *Is she dying right now?*

*No. No,* thought Rimi. *She has the colors of someone with the death sadness, but she has other colors, too. She has the broken webs in her, but the colors around her head are strong and interesting. Travis makes the true colors brighter.*

*Huh.*

"Maya? You okay?" Benjamin asked. Maya's gaze was fixed on the lake and mountain watercolor, on a spot of yellow and orange she realized now was a tiny campfire against the wilderness.

"Just talking to Rimi," Maya said.

"Ah," said Benjamin.

"What about this one?" Gwenda asked. She pointed to a picture on the opposite wall that Maya hadn't noticed before. It showed the silhouette of a woman against a sunset, but the colors in the clouds were a little off, a little too purple and green. The woman had a spear in her right hand, its butt resting against the outside of her foot. The hair flared from her head, indicating wind, and she stood on a cliff above a stormy sea. Green light glowed under the sea's surface of pale froth, and there were . . . shadows of things in the water.

"Good technique," Maya said. "Scary picture. What do you think?"

"This is a Litachi spearhead," said Gwenda, pointing to the spear, which ended in a head shaped with a broad base and a short blade, almost an equilateral triangle, with two small wings at the bottom. "They use those on Fillistrana."

"Where's that?"

"Through a portal."

"Oh. Whoa."

"Wild," said Benjamin. "I think I've seen that cliff, too." He traced the irregular bulge at the lip of the cliff with a finger, not quite touching the surface of the picture. "Fillistrana. That might be a good world for you to visit on your first field trip."

"That's not good for a first stop," Gwenda said. "Too

many hostile others. Maya, I bet you'd like Troana. They have flowers there as big as your head, in all kinds of colors we never see here, and the fairies come from there."

"Troana," Maya whispered. "I'd like to go there."

"I think we have a field trip scheduled there next week," said Benjamin. "We collect a lot of pollen there. People we barter with use it for spice. I bet Aunt Sarutha would let you go."

*No!* Rimi thought. *We are not going through a portal to anywhere!*

*Kachik-Vati went through a portal. Ara-Kita went through a portal. What are you scared of?* Maya thought

*Portaling is bad. It hurts, and people can mess with you. I don't want us going through any portals.*

*Rimi,* Maya began, but she was also afraid at the thought of going through a portal. She wished she had asked Vati or Kachik what it was like. She could ask Benjamin and Gwenda, but they were used to it.

"Okay, folks," Travis called from the other room. "You can join us now."

Maya followed Gwenda into the room, trailed by Benjamin.

It was a pleasant sitting room with big windows. The

floor was hardwood. A crafts table was set up in front of the windows, with several works in progress on it. Some involved paints and canvas. Maya wanted to go check them out, but she held herself back.

A hospital bed stood against the wall nearest the door. In the center of the room was a dining room table with three chairs around it and a gap on the remaining side where a wheelchair could fit. A door in the right wall was ajar, with the sound of water running beyond it, and a door in the left wall was open, revealing a slice of kitchen.

Travis stood beside a small woman in a wheelchair near the dining table. She had waves of silver-blonde hair and bright black eyes. She had gently sagging folds around her eyes and mouth. Her skin looked as soft as peach fuzz. She wore red lipstick and a fluffy mint-green bathrobe. She had furry brown monster slippers with three toe-claws on each foot. "Sorry about that," she said in a robust voice. "Plumbing's an issue for me, and for everybody who takes care of me. I've tried to move beyond embarrassment about it and just get practical, so I hope you children can, too. Who do we have here?"

Travis said, "Oma, this is Maya, Benjamin, and Gwenda. Gwenda, Maya, Benjamin, my grandma. I call her Oma. Oma, what should they call you?"

"You children may call me Oma as well, or if you prefer, you could call me Mrs. Orgelbauer. I'm so pleased to meet Travis's friends." She held out her hand, which looked somehow askew. It was so strange Maya wanted to draw it, even though she thought no one would believe the picture was of a real person's hand. The fingers were swollen and twisted, and Maya wondered if Oma hurt when people touched them.

Benjamin stepped up and gently gripped Oma's hand. "Nice to meet you, Nola."

"Pleased to meet—what did you call me, young man?"

"Nola, I'm Benjamin Porta, and this is my cousin, Gwenda Janus. Maya's an adopted member of our family, and Travis is in training to be a *giri*, though he can't talk about that."

"Oh!" Oma put both hands to her cheeks. "Oh! Oh, my."

"Oma?" Travis said, bending to look her in the face. "Are you okay?"

"All these years. My secret life. I couldn't—I couldn't tell you, Travis." She smiled. "Benjamin. Gwenda. Yes, I believe I've seen you at Janus House."

Benjamin smiled. "Now that I see you, I know I've met you before, too, Oma. Only, when Great-aunt Elia introduced us, she called you something else, didn't she?"

"Of course, of course. Heidi is my first name, but the children all called me Nola." She sat back in her chair and smiled. "Oh, to open my mouth and have words come freely for the first time in ages. I have to appreciate the silence—I might have slipped otherwise, who knows? But it's been hard, too."

Travis said, "Uncle Dude put silence on me, too, and I couldn't talk about it at all—well, hey, now, listen here to what's coming out of my mouth. Did the silence wear off?" He looked at Gwenda.

She shook her head. "Not until he takes it off," she said. "But it has side rules. Maybe, now that Benjamin started talking about Janus House things to your oma, the silence relaxes."

*I wonder if I could take the silence off of Travis*, Rimi thought. *I bet he has the same* squizzles *in the sides of his airtube as you did.*

*Can you fix other people the way you fix me?*

*That's part of what Vati taught me. I can do things for you and I can do them for other people, too. It's a different way, but I know how now.* She sent an arm toward Travis, then drew it back. *Ask him first.*

Oma sniffed. "I'm so happy for you, Travis. I know

you're having a tough time because of me. I'm glad you found magic."

He leaned over and hugged her. Oma couldn't see what Maya saw, the doubt that clouded Travis's brow. He managed to smile before he released his grandmother. "I'm glad I know more about who you are," he said. "Some of the things that have puzzled me for a long time are clearer now. The magic wand? The Doowah Box?"

"Oh, dear," she said. "The Seeker and the Doowah! Elia put a silence on me, but I guess parts of it were permeable. I wasn't supposed to show you those things, but I managed it somehow, I guess by playing pretend." She patted his arm and smiled up at him. "I suppose you could inherit all my tools . . . and my secret room."

"I don't want to inherit anything, Oma. Uh—*what* secret room?"

Oma smiled. "I don't have to die to pass on my knowledge and skills, let alone my tools. I'll tell you how to get to the room. It's upstairs, and I haven't been able to get there since the crash. Benjamin said you're training with someone at Janus House?"

"Yeah, a couple people, actually. Some of what they're teaching me is flat-out weird, and some is way near to normal, like, I'm supposed to study currency exchange. When I ask them why, they smile and shrug."

"A lot of what I did was shopping," said Oma. "They popped me through a portal to Egypt, and then I had to go out and haggle with people at the markets for herbs, or jewelry, or bits of stone or artifacts. Sometimes I had to find a guide who would take me by camel to some specific place to get special sand. Sometimes I had to travel to other parts of Africa and buy things. Sometimes—" She laughed. "I drove up to Canada for something or other—they don't have a portal there. Once I even flew to Mexico City. That was for some special earth. They can do a lot of that by Internet now, but sometimes it takes a known and trusted person to go get it.

"You need to learn exchange rates and local customs and a bit of the language to make those shopping expeditions work out right. And that's where the Doowah Box comes in handy. It's portable protection, a bottomless shopping bag, and it's got a translator in it, too. Oh, my, I'm talking about all these things I've known for ages and couldn't share with anybody, even your opa. It feels so good!

"But where are my manners? Children, please sit. Travis, perhaps our guests would like some tea?" Oma gripped the wheels of her chair and moved it over to the dining table. "Benjamin, the extra chair is against the wall by the bed, if you would be so kind as to fetch it."

Benjamin got the chair and brought it to the table, and everyone sat except Travis, who went through the open door into the kitchen and set a teakettle on a burner, then returned.

"Oh, this is so—" Oma smiled at each of them. "Such a relief."

Then her face fell. She stared at the floor. Her hand opened and closed on the arm of her wheelchair. When she looked up, her eyes were bright with unshed tears. "When Elia died, Harper barred me from Janus house."

# FIFTEEN

"Oh, Oma!" Travis jumped up and hugged her again.

"Did he tell you why?" Gwenda asked.

Oma sniffled and shook her head. "But he never did like me. When Elia proposed me for *giri*, Harper objected. This was years ago, and he wasn't in charge back then—that was old Jerusalah Janus, Harper's daddy. Jerusalah and the Gates sisters voted me in over Harper's objections. I think part of it was that I was a girl, and it was easier for male *giri* to get things done in those days. Some people in other countries wouldn't even talk to me because I was a woman. Elia helped me dress up as a man sometimes. I had such adventures!"

"Was that before you met Opa?" Travis asked.

"Before and after. Poor man, he never knew where I went or why, but he trusted me, and that's a rare thing, I understand. Elia and I made friends with each other in grade school. Harper was a few years older, but he kept trying to talk Elia into breaking off our friendship. Then as now, Janus House folk were not supposed to connect with the community very much. In it, but not of it, they would say. The children were taught that. When I married Isaac, Elia and I had already been friends for years, and all he knew was that I had to go off with her on women's retreats periodically."

The kettle whistled, and Travis went to the kitchen and returned presently with a pot of tea on a tray and five cups. Also a plate of molasses cookies, some napkins, a pitcher of milk, and a sugar bowl. He set it on the table in front of his grandmother and sat down again.

"Thank you, dear." Oma poured tea and passed cups to everyone.

"Oma, I don't think it's right, that Great-uncle Harper banned you from the house," Benjamin said. "Even if he doesn't like you. Did you ever betray us? Did you ever give away our secrets or cause us danger?"

"No," said Oma. "I kept my silence, except when I

played with Travis, and that was a different kind of silence. He never knew my Doowah Box had anything to do with Janus House, did you, honey?"

"Not a ca-lue," said Travis.

Benjamin said, "You should be among our honored."

"Thank you, dear," said Oma.

"It's not right." Benjamin frowned. "I want to talk to Ma about this. Someone should bring it up at the next general meeting. We take care of our own. That's what the adults always tell us, anyway."

Oma smiled at him. "I appreciate your fire, Benjamin. I have let go of it all now. No way I could be a help to you in my current state."

"That's not the point," said Benjamin. "The adults say we should take the long view. We study our own history, and try to use the past to guide us. You are part of our history, and we should respect and honor you. Great-uncle Harper—he—" Benjamin shook his head. "It's not right."

"Well," Oma said. She paused. She stared out the window with a faint smile. "I saw so many wonders and went so many places. I wouldn't have missed it for the world. I have no regrets, my dears, except that I've lost the magic now that I'm trapped in this chair."

"We can bring that back to you," Gwenda said, fingering her bracelet.

Oma smiled even wider. She cocked her head and looked at Maya. "How does one get adopted by those Janus House people? I've never heard of such a thing."

"By accident. A portal person attached to me, and they're making sure I'm taken care of."

"A portal person," Oma said. "Which species? I only met the ones who breathed air. I imagine this is one of those?"

"*Sissimi*," Maya said. Her stomach churned. She was regretting her lost silence now. Oma had to be trustworthy enough to tell a secret to; she'd kept all her Janus House secrets for a long time, even from Travis, but Maya still felt a little uncomfortable talking about it.

"Never heard of that one," said Oma. "Was the detachment painful? Once a *jinjin* suckered onto my arm, and getting it off hurt a lot."

"You met a *jinjin*?" Gwenda said. "I've never even seen one, just heard stories."

"I think the Council restricted portal access to them sometime in the seventies," said Oma. "They had too great an appetite for any kind of flesh they could sucker onto. The diplomatic incidents!" She rolled up the sleeve of her robe on her left arm and showed them a ring of red on her upper arm. "Isaac didn't believe me when I told him an octopus left this mark. That was probably one of our worst fights. He wanted me to stay home after that, if I was going places and tangling with dangerous octopi, or anything else that could hurt me. But I wouldn't stop being a *giri*." She put her hand on Travis's and smiled. "Now I'll have to worry about you, but I'm happy for you, too. So many worlds will open up for you now."

He smiled, then smiled a little wider. "No lie. I hadn't thought much about it. I'm going through portals. Cowabunga."

"Oma, back here on Earth," Gwenda said, "we want to know what you need and how we can help. Travis hasn't told us much about what's going on for you, but we know he's distressed—"

"Now, wait just a danged minute," Travis said.

"Concerned? Busy?" Gwenda suggested.

Travis frowned.

Oma patted Travis's hand. "Yes. I know. I hate being such a burden. I'm used to being the one who helps, and this is painful for me. Travis has been so good to me. I hope you know how much I appreciate it, Trav. Oh, dear.

If you're going to be a *giri*, you'll need to get away more—"

Travis said, "I've told you before, stop it with the burden thing, okay, Oma? Anyway, they say I don't have any *giri* duties until I get some training. I'm getting training in my free period after school, except when Artemis has to take off early. But it will probably take a while."

"Ah."

"We have several family members studying elder care who would like to practice on you," Gwenda said.

Oma's brows drew together in a frown. "Practice what?"

"Caring."

"Oh, I couldn't—it's not a thing you share with strangers—oh. Well, no, I suppose I could," she said, looking sideways at Travis. "It would help if there were people to spell you, wouldn't it?"

"I never asked for that," said Travis. "You know I love you, Oma."

"Love doesn't stop you from burning out. I hate to be a charity case. . . . I guess that's arrogant of me, isn't it? If you're telling me true, Gwenda girl, then I say send them on over and let's get to know one another."

"It's not charity if you've earned it, ma'am," said Benjamin. "You've been a *giri* for a long time. We owe you."

"You'd be helping them learn, too, Oma," Gwenda said.

Oma smiled. "When you put it that way—I'd be churl-
ish to refuse. Thank you."

Maya stood up. "Oma, do you paint?"

"Yes, I do," said Oma.

"Did you do the art in the hallway?"

"Indeed I did. Isaac used to trouble himself about my
imagination. 'You know you've given that sheep too many
horns,' he'd say, or, 'Those folk are too thin to be real.' I'd
tell him it was a place I'd visited in my imagination. It worried him a little, but he put up with it."

"Do you ever teach art?"

"Teach art? I'm self-taught myself. I don't want to train
other people to make my mistakes."

"Oma," Maya said.

*Show her your sketchbook*, Rimi thought.

Maya pulled her sketchbook out of her backpack and
opened it to her most recent drawing. She had drawn
Kachik-Vati yesterday, with Rimi's help, when they were in
the hideout in the woods with Travis. She held up the picture to show Oma.

"Oh," Oma said. "Oh! Oh, you're very skillful! And—
there's something—" She held out her arms, and Maya
laid the sketchbook across them. Oma frowned down at

the picture. Gwenda and Benjamin stood to look over her shoulders.

"That's the *mrudim* you met yesterday?" Gwenda asked.

"Kachik," said Maya, and then she pointed to the extra arm. "Vati."

"There's something about the technique," Oma said. She tapped her index finger on the fur. "I don't understand how you got the swirls in the fur here."

"Oma, you asked me about the portal person who attached to me. This person, Rimi, is still part of me. She drew the swirls, and I did most of the other work on the picture. Both of us want to learn more about art. If you would teach us, we wouldn't have to worry about being sneaky. When Rimi draws, it's—not what people expect to see. Could you help us? Could we come here for art lessons?"

"Well, I don't—" Oma said. She looked at her work table, then at Travis. He smiled at her. "I don't—" She paused, took a breath. Set Maya's sketchbook on the table. "I don't see why not," she said at last. "Except that I don't know I have anything to teach you."

"It might be enough if I could come here and draw for an hour or two without worrying about having to hide the pictures, or the way Rimi and I do them."

"Rimi is still attached to you."

"I think we're bonded for life." Maya retrieved her sketchpad, got out two pencils, and opened to a fresh page. "Here." She started outlining a picture of Travis's face. Rimi picked up the other pencil and roughed in his hair, a bit shaggy and shoulder-length, touching down lightly to keep the color bright instead of shady. Maya put ovals for his eyes to get their placement, then worked on drawing one eye while Rimi drew the other. Both she and Rimi kept glancing at Travis until he got nervous. She put a line where his nose went and another for his mouth, and Rimi drew his jaw line, and then they both worked on adding the details that made Travis uniquely himself.

Oma stared at Rimi's pencil, working without a visible agent.

Maya and Rimi dropped their pencils at the same time, and Rimi lifted the sketchpad from Maya's hands and turned it so Oma could see the picture.

Travis blushed and put his hand over his face.

Oma drew in a breath. "May I have it?"

"Sure," said Maya. Rimi pulled the picture out of the sketchbook and gently placed it in Oma's hand.

"Rimi?" Oma said.

Rimi patted Oma's cheek.

Oma smiled. "Thank you, dear." She closed her eyes.

Rimi patted her cheek twice more and withdrew. Oma sighed and opened her eyes. "I don't know that I have anything to teach either of you, but you would be welcome to come and spend an afternoon doing art with me."

"Have you worked with oils?" Maya asked.

"Not successfully. I've had fun with acrylics, but mostly, as you saw in the front hall, I work in charcoal, pastel, and watercolor."

"I'd like to try all those things," said Maya. She mostly worked with pencils and crayons, occasionally trying watercolors. Her teacher in Idaho had been working with Maya on her pencil portraits of people. Before she'd found her Idaho teacher, Maya had worked on her own mostly, although she and Peter had had some classes from a friend of their mother's who had given them stacks of things to make collages out of.

*Tell her it doesn't matter what we work on, as long as we can work,* Rimi said, so Maya repeated that. "My parents will pay you," Maya added.

"Bless you, child, I don't need money."

"They'll want to, though, because then it will make sense that I'm coming over here. Oma . . . this will be great for me. Is it something you'd like to do?"

Oma looked at the sketch of Travis, then studied Maya

with her head cocked sideways. "Yes," she said. "Very much."

"Could I come to class as well, Oma?" Gwenda asked.

"Why—" Oma sat back and laid her hands in her lap. "Yes."

Benjamin raised his hand. Travis did, too. "Oma, I wish I'd thought of this before," Travis said.

"You're going to have to help me with supplies," Oma said.

"We can all do that," said Benjamin.

Oma smiled. "So are you thinking Tuesday afternoons?"

Maya exchanged glances with Travis, Gwenda, and Benjamin.

"We don't have training on Tuesdays and Thursdays," Travis said, "so Tuesdays would work for me."

"Me, too," said Maya. "I have piano lessons on Thursday."

"We have to talk to our teachers," Gwenda said.

"And Great-uncle Harper. Or maybe Aunt Noona," said Benjamin.

"Aunt Noona." Gwenda nodded.

"All right," said Oma. "Let me know who can come. The first thing we're going to need is a sketch pad for each of you. Then tools of choice. Let's put together a list."

# SIXTEEN

Maya told her parents at supper that she had found an art teacher.

"Who is it?" asked her mother.

"My friend Travis's grandmother."

"Travis is the tall, good-looking one who isn't from Janus House, right?" Candra said.

"Right," said Maya.

"We'll need to meet her," Dad said.

"Sure," said Maya. "She lives about three blocks away."

"This is exciting, honey," said her mother.

"Yeah." Maya smiled.

Someone knocked at the front door when Maya and

Peter were washing up after dinner, and Candra went to answer it. Maya heard murmurs, and then Candra came back to the kitchen, where Mom and Dad had settled at the table with homework they needed to check, and Candra had set out her math homework.

"Evren's here," Candra said. "He wants to go for a walk with me. Is that okay?"

"How nice of you to ask," Dad said. Maya couldn't tell whether he was being sarcastic.

Mom stood up. "Evren. Evren. A faint bell rings. Could you ask him to step in here?"

Candra turned to talk to the person behind her. "I told you they'd want to see you," she said.

"And I said that's fine," said Evren, stepping past Candra into the kitchen. "Evening, Mrs. Andersen, Mr. Andersen." He wore jeans and a blue windbreaker, and his shoulders were hunched. He looked beautiful.

"Evren Janus," said Mom. "Now I remember."

"I've got a forgettable face."

"I wouldn't say that," Mom said, "but you keep a low profile."

*Forgettable face,* Rimi thought. *Ha! He makes people forget his face.*

*Let's draw him,* Maya thought. She dried her hands on a dishtowel and grabbed the current sketchpad out of her backpack, which was waiting by the kitchen table for her to finish the dishes and get to her homework.

"Maya," Peter protested. There were still dirty dishes in the dishpan. He was drying the dishes after she washed them, so he was stuck if she left in the middle.

"In a minute." She sat at the table, opened to a blank page, and sketched in the basics of Evren's face, then added detail. When she glanced up at him again, he smiled at her and worked his fingers in a pattern she didn't recognize. When she looked down at the page, the drawing she had started was gone.

Evren winked at her.

*How did he do that?* Maya asked Rimi.

*Let me see.* A faint shadow moved over the page. *Spinners and shifters! So elegant! Little buzzers came and lifted the lines off, but the push-down is still here.*

Maya touched the page through the shadow. She could still feel the depressions left by her pressure on the pencil. If she shaded across the page, the way people always did in mystery movies to get clues, she was pretty sure she would find the picture again, only it would look like a negative.

"It's a school night," Dad said to Candra and Evren. "You can go out for a little while, but I'd appreciate it if you were back by ten."

"Sure," said Candra.

"No problem," said Evren.

"Later," said Candra, and they both headed out, with a brief pause by the front coat closet for Candra to grab her coat. The front door slammed with a puff of cool air moving through the house.

*I can un*twizz *this*, Rimi thought, focused on the disappeared drawing. Her shadow grew thicker across the paper; glitter sparkled in it, and then silvery grains filled in the lines Maya had drawn, and Evren's image was there on the page again, shinier than before.

*Thanks, Rimi! What is it filled with?*

*I polished the pencil stuff a little.* Rimi thought a smile.

*Nice.*

"So that's probably a good sign," Dad said to Mom. "She's found some kind of boyfriend. I would have thought it would be someone from high school, though."

"Someone from next door," Mom said. "Might be easier."

"Maya, you spend a lot of time at Janus House," Dad said. "We see them every Saturday night, and I have to admire their musicianship, but I feel I don't know much else about them."

"Dr. Porta is a terrific baker," Mom said.

"Well, there is that." Dad tapped a pencil against the table a few times. "If this thing with Candra gets serious, though, I want to see where Evren lives. Does he have parents? If he does, who are they? Maya, do you know anything about his family?"

Maya shook her head. She closed her sketchbook on Rimi's rendering of her Evren drawing and went back to the sink. "I don't remember much about him," she said. "We met him when we went over to see Gwenda's closet."

"Is he related to Gwenda?"

"Same last name," Maya said. "A lot of people over there are related to each other."

"Is he Gwenda's big brother?"

"I don't think so."

"Well, it might amount to nothing," Dad said, and he and Mom bent back to their work.

Maya tested Rimi's alarm clock capabilities the next morning. Rimi shook her awake, not just on the shoulder, but all through her. Maya felt like a bowl of jiggling Jell-O. She snapped her eyes open. "Ow?" she said, experimentally.

*Did I hurt you? I was careful!*

"It doesn't hurt, it just feels weird." Maya sat up and looked at the clock. "It's fifteen minutes before I wanted to wake up."

*I didn't want to wait any more,* Rimi thought. *It always takes you longer than you think.*

"Okay," Maya said. She got up. Rimi had already put her homework and art supplies in her backpack. "Whoa. Thanks, Rimi." Maya dressed, pulled on her pack, and headed out into the hall. She almost collided with Peter.

"So you were always talking to Rimi," he whispered.

"My shadow," she whispered back. "Were you listening at my door?"

"No, just on my way downstairs." He had his school backpack on, too, and his shoelaces were untied.

"Hey, you could trip—" Maya said, and then Rimi tied Peter's shoelaces.

"Oh, wow," he said.

She put extra knots in the laces.

"But I won't be able to get them off," he said.

*Ask me and I'll untie them,* Rimi thought.

Maya relayed the message.

"Yeah, but you're not at my school. I'll need to change for P.E."

Rimi paused, then undid the outermost layer of knots.

"What are you guys talking about now?" Candra said, breezing past them on her way to the stairs.

"Peter's shoelaces," Maya said. "Hey, how'd your walk with Evren go last night?"

"Wouldn't you like to know?" Candra was gone down the stairs.

"Yes!" Maya yelled, following her. Peter was on her heels. They all headed for the kitchen.

It was Cold Cereal Day. Mom and Dad were already sitting at the table drinking coffee. Candra grabbed a box of cereal from the lineup on the counter and poured some in a bowl, added milk, and started scarfing. Peter poured a pile of ChocoNut Bits into a bowl. Maya got honey-nut cereal for herself.

"What happened last night?" Maya asked Candra again.

Candra just smiled and ate. Then she said, "Live in ignorance, the way you made me live all these weeks."

"Candra, where did you and Evren go?" Mom asked.

"Just around a few blocks, Mom. There were streetlights

all the way." She hunched her shoulders. "This is our neighborhood now. I don't want to be scared of it. I don't have to, do I?"

"No," said Dad. "As far as we know, this is a safe place to live and wander."

"Good." She finished her cereal and rinsed out her bowl, then stuck it in the dishwasher.

"Did you kiss?" Peter asked.

"What? Of course not," Candra said, blushing. "All we did was talk."

"What about?" Peter demanded.

"That is seriously none of your business, squirt," she said, then relented. "We mostly talked about me. I didn't notice until after we said good night. I had so many questions for him, but somehow, he sidetracked me into talking about me. Next time I'm going to change that."

"There's a next time?" Maya asked.

"There will be." Candra settled her messenger bag over her shoulder. "Dad?"

"Sit down, Candra. I'm not leaving until I've finished my coffee."

Candra frowned and sat down, but her posture was tense. She jiggled one leg.

"That's not going to make me drink any faster," Dad

said, and focused on the newspaper he was reading.

Maya ate quietly and got up. She put her lunch in her backpack and went to the door. *No rush rush, Rimi. I might be able to get used to this. Thanks again.*

*Time is easy to watch, but not always interesting,* Rimi thought.

"See you later, everybody," Maya said, and left.

Aunt Sarutha sat on the Janus House porch again, weaving something about six inches wide, and this time Maya walked over to her. "Morning, Namdi. Did the others leave already?"

"No," Sarutha said. She smiled. "Maya, would you skip singing class this afternoon and stop at Columba's apartment instead? I'll be by to pick you up. I shouldn't be too late, if all goes according to plan."

"Sure," Maya said.

Sarutha rummaged in a bag beside her, then held up a square of material. It looked thick and stiff and dark, and it had a picture picked out in colored thread. A quick look showed Maya three figures that looked humanoid but not human. "Here's some homework for you and Rimi. See what you can learn from studying it. I'll leave it with Columba for you."

Rimi stretched out a limb and touched the material.

Something thrummed through her, reaching Maya less than a second later. Maya's teeth felt jiggly. "What—Namdi—"

"No peeking!" Sarutha said. She tucked the square of cloth back into her bag and shook her index finger at Maya.

Then Benjamin, Gwenda, Rowan, Kallie, and Twyla burst out of the front doors and swept Maya up with them in the rush to get to school on time.

In social studies class, Rimi poked Maya. *That Sibyl is looking at you again.*

Maya glanced up from her textbook. Sibyl was two rows in front of Maya and Travis. They had settled in the back row in this class without the excuse of Janus House kids, and sometimes Maya was sorry they'd picked these seats. She liked Mr. Harrison as a teacher. He made American history interesting, and he was funny. Occasionally he was mean when somebody wasn't paying attention, and once in a while, that was Maya. But for the most part, she had a good time in his class.

She hadn't noticed Sibyl particularly until this week, and this week she was only noticing Sibyl because Sibyl seemed to be noticing Maya first.

Mr. Harrison had his back to them. He was writing on

the board about the causes of revolution. With his attention distracted, Sibyl had turned most of the way around in her seat to stare through her glasses at Maya. She was wearing a dark red dress today, but she had the same golden scarf around her neck. It was the prettiest thing about her.

*Gwenda thinks there's something off about her,* Maya thought. *Can you sense it?*

Rimi stretched along the floor, edging closer to Sibyl. She paused before she reached the girl. *The air is* pattishaw, she thought.

*What does that mean?*

*Something is wrinkly in it.* Rimi retreated, tightened around Maya. *It makes me* burizz.

*Weird.*

Travis tapped her arm. She glanced toward him. He'd written a note in the margin of his notebook. *What's up?*

Maya wrote a note on the edge of her notebook. *Don't know.*

They both shrugged, and then Mr. Harrison turned around and stared right at them, as though he knew they hadn't been paying attention.

Rimi focused on Sibyl the rest of class, but nothing else happened.

*She smells wrong,* Rimi thought after the bell rang and

everyone rose to go to their next class. *She smells—she* sist*is strange. Or maybe something else is familiar in a strange way.*

*You watch her while I'm watching the school stuff?* Maya thought.

*Yes.*

# SEVENTEEN

As Maya followed Travis and the Janus House kids home from school following last period, Rimi nudged her. *Still watching*, she said. Maya glanced back and saw Sibyl leaning against the wall of the school, her head turned away as though nothing could be more fascinating than the trees across the road, with their few rags of colored leaves still dangling.

*I'll have to talk to her sometime, I guess*, Maya thought. *Let me know if she follows us.*

*All right.* Rimi got distracted just then, though, by something in a trash can they were passing. She had to taste it, and Maya got a fragment of the taste.

*Eww. What is that?*

*I don't know. It's purple and squishy.*

*Overshare!* Maya swallowed a few times, then broke out a piece of mint gum. She chomped furiously.

In the front hall of Janus House, everyone split up. Travis headed upstairs to study with his teachers. Gwenda, Benjamin, Kallie, Twyla, and Rowan also headed upstairs, for singing class. Maya knocked on Columba's door.

Columba's door opened. So did the door to Benjamin's apartment. Dr. Porta came out, a bulging tapestry bag over her shoulder. "Hi, Maya," she said as she crossed the front hall toward them. "I heard you were at loose ends this afternoon. I want to try an experiment to find out more about your *sissimi*."

Maya stilled. *Do we want her to find out more about you?* she wondered.

*I'm always curious*, Rimi thought.

*She might uncover our secrets.*

*She might uncover secrets about us we don't know yet. I love secrets*, thought Rimi.

"Namdi Sarutha left me some homework," Maya said.

"That's okay. My experiment won't take much of your attention. Hey, Columba. Okay if I come in, too?"

"Okay," said Columba. "I'm still not sure about this

entertaining business. You know more about it than I do. But Maya, I actually got you some bread this time."

"Good thinking," Dr. Porta said. "Is it some of mine?"

"From the batch of banana bread you made this morning," Columba said.

"One of my better batches," said Dr. Porta. She smiled. "They're all good, though. Maya, you'll eat, won't you?"

"Yes. Thanks!" Maya stared down at her stomach. It growled, on cue.

"What would you like to drink, Maya? Sapphira? Tea?" asked Columba.

"I guess, as long as it's not chamomile," Maya said.

"Come on in." Columba turned, and Maya followed her into the apartment, through the living room, and into the kitchen. Dr. Porta came, too.

"What kind of tea would either of you like?" Columba filled an orange kettle with water and put it on the stove to boil.

"Peppermint," Maya said. "Do you have that?"

"Mm." Columba opened a cupboard. Maya saw a bunch of different types of teas there. Columba picked a pink box and closed the cupboard. "Sapphira, you okay with peppermint?"

"Sure, sure." Dr. Porta put her satchel on the floor and

took out a blue crystal bowl, a clear glass rod, and some cloth zipper pouches. She set the bowl on one end of the kitchen table, produced a water bottle from the satchel, and mixed things in the bowl. She sang softly in Kerlinqua while she worked, timing the strokes of the glass rod with the beat of her song. Maya didn't recognize any words except *girana*, which meant *make or do*, and three other verbs that just confused her.

Columba ran water in the kitchen sink. When it was steaming, she filled a white and blue porcelain teapot and set it beside the sink to warm.

"Maya, have a seat." Columba gestured toward the kitchen table. "You can do your homework here."

"Thanks," Maya said. She dropped into the chair farthest from Dr. Porta's mixing station and settled her pack next to her, then got the sketchpad and pencils out. Maybe she should try drawing a picture of Sibyl. If she drew Sibyl, she might understand her better.

But wait a minute, she could also draw what was right in front of her. She flipped the sketchpad open, grabbed a couple of pencils, and drew Dr. Porta mixing. Dr. Porta had wild, wavy black hair, and her black eyes looked slightly mad as she worked with the ingredients she took out of her bag. Maya emphasized the mad scientist look in the drawing.

"Maya, Benjamin tells me there's a mysterious store near-by," Columba said. "How long have you known about it?"

"Since we moved here. I didn't realize it was mysterious, though, except the owner kind of creeps me out. I haven't gone inside since before Rimi."

"I've sent some of my minions to investigate. It seems to be warded against us, though. If you do go in, could you bring me back your impressions?"

"Sure," said Maya.

"Excellent. Could you draw me a picture of the owner?"

"I guess." Maya turned to a fresh page. She had just seen him through the window the day before, but there was something about him that made her turn and look other directions. Frowning, she thought about that. That was when she should pay more attention, she decided, when things were pushing her eyes somewhere else. She drew the heavy dark brows overshadowing the deep-set eyes, the long hair pulled back into a braid, the stark bones of his cheeks and jawline, then tore the sketch from her pad and handed it to Columba. Dr. Porta finished stirring and looked over Columba's shoulder.

"Hmm," said Columba. "Thanks, Maya." She filed the sketch in a drawer.

Maya turned the page and did a sketch of Sibyl and

her scarf, then flipped another page and drew a picture of Stephanie.

*Who am I going to be for Halloween this year, Steph?* she thought. *Who can I be?*

Last year Stephanie had been a Rapunzel princess out of her tower, and Maya had been her ghostly friend and companion. Maya had covered her face with white grease paint and used dark greasepaint to make circles around her eyes, add hollows to her cheeks, and blacken her lips. She had found several lengths of pale gauzy material to drape over black jeans and a black shirt, and she had practiced ghost noises. Her mother helped her safety-pin the gauze to her other clothes so it stayed in place. She draped a big piece over her head.

Stephanie had had that crazy wig, curly blonde hair down to her ankles, and she wore a dress with lots of sequins that she and Maya had glued to it in a pattern Maya had designed. She put rhinestone star clips in her fake hair, and she carried a magic wand with a glowing crystal at the tip.

Her cheeks had looked gaunt. Princess makeup couldn't disguise her weight loss. Steph smiled so much, and seemed so cheerful, that Maya could almost pretend the chemo didn't make her too nauseated to eat for three days after each treatment. Maya sat with Steph in her bedroom after school on days when Steph was too sick to come to school and talked about what they had learned that day, and played cards with her, and drew her pictures, and Steph just made up stories and smiled, so Maya thought maybe things weren't that bad. Steph went through periods between treatments where she seemed like her old self.

Last Halloween, they had started out strong, walking the same neighborhood they had toured every Halloween since they were three and clinging to their parents' hands. They knew which houses were likely to give full-size candy bars, which ones gave you a toothbrush instead of a treat, which people were likely to dress up to answer the door for trick-or-treaters. Maya liked saving the best houses for last.

But that night, she and Stephanie had only gone two blocks when Stephanie faltered. "I'm sorry, my shady friend," Stephanie had said. She stopped, holding onto the hood of a parked car. "I'm tired already. I know that's not very princess-y of me."

"We can't stop now. The Halvorsons. The Flynns. The Harrises," Maya said.

Stephanie was breathing loudly. "I'm sorry," she said

again. She turned away and leaned against the car, hanging onto the roof as though it were the only thing keeping her on her feet. "I'm sorry, Maya. Just now the magic left me."

All that candy uncollected, Maya had thought, visions of Snickers and Milky Ways and Reese's Peanut Butter Cups dancing through her mind, and then she sighed. "Okay," she said. "Can you make it home?"

Stephanie didn't speak for a little while. The cool night was quiet except for her heavy breathing. Candles flickered in pumpkins on a nearby porch, and distant trick-or-treaters were running silhouettes under an orange street-light down at the corner. Woodsmoke flavored the air.

"I think I better call Daddy," Steph said, and got out her cell phone.

After the call, Maya put her arm around Stephanie's waist and helped her over to the lawn in front of the Collins' house. There was a bench there. Steph sat down, hugging her loot bag, her head down and the Rapunzel hair shielding her. Maya sat beside her and stared toward the street. When Steph started to sniffle, Maya took her hand. "It's all right," she whispered. "It's all right. It's all right."

For the first time, Maya had asked herself, *What if she doesn't get better?*

Stephanie had lived until spring.

Rimi stroked Maya's back as Maya sat with her pencil tip digging into the picture of Stephanie. Steph stared out of the page at Maya. She looked like she had before the cancer diagnosis, smiling and healthy, full of mischief. *Find your secret self,* she had said more than once, and Maya heard her saying it again.

*Am I your secret self?* Rimi asked.

*I don't know how secret you are when a house full of people know about you, plus Peter,* thought Maya. *And anyway, you're your own self.*

*Where is your secret self?*

*My secret self keeps changing,* Maya thought. *Stephanie had lots of secret selves, and mine were always boring compared to hers. She thought up the best stories.*

*Stories are everywhere,* Rimi thought. *What story do you like right now?*

*I like the story of a girl meeting an alien and being best friends,* Maya thought. She felt a pang. Best friends. She and Steph had sworn they were forever friends. Steph wouldn't have wanted Maya not to have any other friends, though. Magic users and aliens. If only Steph could have been here—

Maya straightened and laid her pencil on the table. *Let's*

*go to a store later and see what kind of secret selves they're selling this year.* Usually Maya's mother helped her assemble a costume, and she was sure they could do it again this year, but it was only four days until Halloween, and Mom hadn't even mentioned it yet.

Maybe she was remembering last year and waiting for Maya to say something.

Columba sliced the loaf of banana bread onto a wooden board and set it on the table between Maya and where Dr. Porta was mixing up her concoction. "Sapphira, what on earth are you making?" she asked Dr. Porta.

Maya helped herself to three slices of bread. It was so moist it didn't even leave crumbs, really. Anything that fell off, Maya could pick up by pressing her finger to it. Sweet, soft, and delicious, banana and cinnamon and ginger. "Oh, this is so good," Maya said.

"Thanks, Maya. Columba, I'm working on a visibility potion," said Dr. Porta. She took a pinch of something bright yellow-green from one of her pouches, rubbed it between finger and thumb, and dropped it into the mix. She stirred the mixture with the glass rod, then dug something that looked like clear jelly from a pocket of her satchel and droobled half a handful into the mix. Faint blue flames sprang up from the mixture, and a smell like lemons and burnt sugar came from it. Dr. Porta stirred harder. The flames winked out. "Okay," she said.

"Are you sure that's what you made?" Columba said. "I don't remember doing it like that in class."

"It's my own recipe. Works better than the one we learned." She dug a golden tablespoon from the satchel and dipped up a spoonful of the mixture. It looked like clear jelly with dark veins in it, and it smelled a little like lemon pie filling. "Here, Maya."

"You first." Maya scooted her chair away from Dr. Porta.

"Um?" Dr. Porta frowned at the wobbly jelly, then put it in her mouth. She pulled out the bare spoon and swallowed. A halo of gemlike golden lights flared around her. "Eh?" Dr. Porta reached for some of the blinking gleams. They darted away from her fingers while maintaining their connection with the other glittering beads of light that surrounded her like a vertical equator. "What on earth?"

Columba laughed just as the teakettle whistled. She took the kettle off the burner, emptied the teapot of the water that had warmed it, put several teabags with their strings twisted together into the pot, and poured hot water on them. Then she turned back to Dr. Porta, who was still chasing the lights. "Don't you know your own signature?"

"This is my signature?"

"Or part of it, anyway." Columba made a triangle with her fingers and thumbs and spoke a soft chant, then looked through her frame at Dr. Porta. "You've left out the other colors. Interesting."

"Nola Columba, what are you doing?" Maya asked.

Columba turned toward Maya, still peering at the triangle she had made of index fingers and thumbs. "Whoa! Wow! That's what Rimi looks like?"

"Huh?" Maya asked.

Columba dropped her hands. "It's a viewing portal for seeing truths not apparent," she said.

"Could you teach me that?"

Columba frowned. "It depends on what abilities you were born with," she said. "Has Sarutha done a power inventory on you yet?"

"I don't know. She asked me questions and wrote things down, but I'm not sure it was a power inventory."

"Well, sooner or later, someone should do one. I'll check with Sarutha. If she hasn't done it, I will."

"Columba, you try this stuff. I can't do a viewing portal. This is the only way I know how to see someone else's powers." Dr. Porta spooned up more of her mixture. She extended it to Columba.

"What the heck." Columba took the spoon and ate what was on it. "Wah! Nice flavor," she said. Tiny angels of many-colored light flickered into sight around her. Or maybe they weren't angels, but tiny glowing lilies, foxgloves, and upended irises, or just some other interesting shapes and colors. They spun and danced around Columba in all directions. Maya sketched as quickly as she could, challenging herself to draw what was in front of her instead of trying to make it conform to something she already knew. She didn't understand what any of these things revealed about Columba, let alone what Dr. Porta's surround of light beads meant, but someone might know. She wished she had brought her colored pencils. She was sure the colors carried information, too. She wrote in color names next to the shapes she sketched.

Columba poured three mugs of tea and set them on the table. Her flower-pixie shapes fluttered here and there as she did it, some of them lighting on the table or the teapot, some hovering, and some racing each other around Columba.

"So is this your signature?" Dr. Porta asked Columba.

Columba looked down through her triangled fingers and thumbs, sang a short song, and frowned. "Most of it. You've left off the shadow end."

"Hmm. I need to tinker with the formula some more. But for now . . . Maya?" Dr. Porta offered her a spoonful of the jelly.

*Here goes*, Maya thought, and ate it before Rimi could comment or object. The flavor was sharp and sweet, lemon with overtones of strawberry, something else she didn't recognize, and just a hint of pepper. Rimi slipped a thread of herself into Maya's mouth before Maya swallowed. As Maya swallowed she felt Rimi withdraw and sensed that Rimi had tasted the stuff, too, but in a different way.

*Interesting*, Rimi thought. *New kind of power in it. I want.*

Rimi appeared, forced out of shadow into bright color, a solid blanket of blue, silver, gray, and green wrapping around Maya, leaving only her face bare, with spikes and waves rising up here and there, and parts of her lapping across the floor in thin rivulets.

"*Kiri kara!*" Dr. Porta said. "So big and solid-looking! And spread out. Is she there like that all the time?"

Columba peered through triangle fingers, then lowered them, then lifted them to look again. "Yep, that's what I just saw. Weird."

"So big," Dr. Porta repeated, staring at the floor, where Rimi rivers in blending shades of greens, grays, blues, and yellows snaked off in different directions. She leaned over and touched a rivulet near her foot. Her finger sank through it. "Hardly even a shiver," she muttered, and leaned closer to look at the parts of Rimi draped over Maya's back.

Maya hugged herself, feeling the snuggle of Rimi against her, as she almost always did. Then she spread her arms and looked down at herself, enveloped in layers of colorful Rimi. The visual representation gave Maya strange feelings. She had drawn pictures of how she imagined Rimi would look, and this Rimi was different, which made her wonder which Rimi was real. She closed her eyes, feeling the Rimi she always felt. It reassured her. She opened her eyes again and set her mind on memorize, but it was hard to memorize, the way Rimi kept shifting color and shape, and with so much of her behind Maya, or too close to see.

Dr. Porta pulled a digital camera from the satchel and shot picture after picture.

Maya stood and held her hands out, turned them up and down. Colors changed across Rimi's prickly surface, and parts of her retracted and expanded, stretched and shrank. Violet flared, followed by orange and red, then different shades of green and blue and some brown. Rimi's pseudopods reached out to the pale orchids in Columba's living room and seemed to be sipping from them. Other extensions branched off to visit other flowers.

A slender Rimi tentacle slid across the table to the bowl containing Dr. Porta's mixture, sneaking up to it on the side away from where Dr. Porta and Columba stood studying Maya and Rimi. Its tip slid up the side of the bowl and into the mixture. Maya felt Rimi tasting the mixture even more thoroughly than she had when it was in Maya's mouth, sorting out individual ingredients and assigning them descriptors, code words that let her think about them in useful ways. *Song stuff,* Rimi thought. *Can't unassemble or rebuild that part. Forgot to record it when she was doing it. I wonder if we can get her to make more so we can catch that part. Could you sing it? I don't know. Your singing doesn't seem to work the way the Janus House people's singing does.*

*Could you make this?* Maya wondered.

*Don't know where some parts come from,* Rimi thought, withdrawing from the bowl. *Know their* scentastes *now, but not sure where to find them. Plus, song component is important.*

Maya wondered what Rimi would do with the potion if she made more. She raised her arm and thought, *Can you make a hand without being attached to me?*

The forest-and-olive-green part of Rimi circling Maya's arm stretched out and made a hand of its own, with eight fingers and a big thumb. The fingers wiggled. The thumb flexed. The hand made a fist, then opened and waved at Maya. Maya laughed. *Can you pick stuff up with that?*

Rimi reached out and picked up a sugar bowl from the kitchen counter beside Columba. "Whoa," Columba said, while Dr. Porta kept shooting. Rimi brought the sugar bowl to the table and scooped a couple of spoonfuls of sugar into Maya's tea.

"Whoa," Columba said again. "That's—"

"Wait a sec. She can lift things?" Dr. Porta said.

"Evidently," said Columba.

"The equivalent of levitation. This means—" She shot a picture of the sugar bowl and Rimi's spoon handling.

"Means what?" Columba asked.

"Means I have something to report," said Dr. Porta.

Rimi set down the spoon, formed a second hand, and rubbed her hands together. Dr. Porta took a picture of that, too. Maya felt Rimi's mental smile.

*Did you always know you could do that?* Maya asked, touching the abandoned spoon.

*I knew I could pick things up. Dirty laundry and guinea*

*pigs. Forks and pencils. I knew I could make a hand that was attached to you, but that was different. Making a hand out of the regular me, that's new,* Rimi thought.

The lights around Dr. Porta winked out. The dancing colored flowers surrounding Columba vanished. Rimi retracted all her extensions and used her arms to hug Maya just before the color faded from her and she went back to being a shadow.

"Good one, Sapphira," Columba said. "Can I keep some of that for later?"

"Sure. Short shelf life on it, though. Use it in the next couple of weeks and then toss it. It turns into something dire after that."

"How can I tell when?"

Dr. Porta looked at the jelly. "It goes a bit mossy, gray and green. Then you don't want to feed it to anybody. Makes you break out in bug hives."

"Ick." Columba got a jar from a cupboard and ladled potion into it, then screwed the top on. "Refrigerate it?"

"Yeah, that helps," said Dr. Porta.

Columba fished a pen out of a drawer and wrote on the jar, then stuck it into the refrigerator. "Fun at parties," she said.

Dr. Porta laughed, then shook her head.

"What would happen if somebody normal ate that?" Maya asked.

"I'm not sure. Are you thinking of feeding it to the *giri* boy?"

"I wasn't, but—"

"It wouldn't hurt him," Dr. Porta said. Then she looked at the ceiling and sucked on her lower lip. "Well . . . I'd want to be there just in case. Everyone has hidden depths. I wonder if it would show any of his?"

"Maya," Columba said, "I'd like to talk to you seriously about a job."

"A job?"

"Yes. You know I run security for Janus House, and I have several people who work with me and one apprentice. *Sissimi* partners are popular with security forces, for reasons that are becoming apparent to me. Istar Harper will be asking you about specializing in something soon, and I'd like to get my request in early. Please give it serious thought, okay?"

"But I—" Maya had had summer jobs weeding gardens, babysitting, walking dogs, watering plants, running errands for her parents, but she didn't want to *work* work right now.

School was her job, she figured. At least, that was what her parents told her.

Now she had two other families. She wondered if Benjamin and Gwenda and Rowan had jobs.

"Just think about it," Columba said.

"Okay."

A knock sounded on the apartment door.

"No, not yet," muttered Dr. Porta. "I have other tests to run."

Sarutha opened the door and peered in. "I'm finished with my other task," she said. "Maya, are you ready to come with me?"

"I didn't even start the homework you gave me," Maya said.

"Oh, right," said Columba. "I forgot to give it to you. Here." She handed a manila envelope to Maya. Maya rose, tucked the envelope into her sketchpad, and put her possessions in her pack. She gulped her tea before she realized it wasn't peppermint, but something that tasted like flowers. It was like drinking perfume with sugar in it. She set down the mug and rubbed her tongue against the roof of her mouth, trying to erase the taste. "You call that peppermint?" she asked Columba.

"Did I mislabel those?" Columba sipped her tea and grimaced. "Sorry. Oh, dear. This is tell-all tea."

"You gave it to us on purpose, didn't you?" Maya asked.

"Yes, I did." Columba set her own mug down and glared at it. "Didn't mean to say that."

"What else have you done to us?" asked Maya.

"That's all. Oh, the orchids, but I forgot I used those. They work on everyone."

"What do the orchids do?"

*I know,* Rimi thought.

"They have a comfort scent," Columba said. She glared at her mug, flicked one index finger across the other toward it. The tea in her mug sizzled and hissed into an upwelling of steam.

*Is that what they do?* Maya asked Rimi.

*They are very friendly. They make you feel safe. They relax you. They taught me how to do that. I think it will be good for us.*

*Make me relax so much I forget to keep my own secrets?* Maya thought.

*Oh. Maybe.* Rimi sent a slender tendril of self into the side of Maya's mouth. *I'll turn the tea off.*

Faint pressure on Maya's tongue, as though a leaf lay

there. A few tiny darts of sparkling pain in her mouth and throat. Maya took a deep breath and breathed out perfume.

*Think I got it before it got too far into you,* Rimi said. *Ask her more questions.*

"What are your other plans for us?" Maya asked.

"General watchfulness and caution," Columba said, "and taking whatever openings you offer. Stop that!"

Dr. Porta poured the tea in her cup out into the sink. "Intriguing," she said. "Col, fifteen years ago, did you try to steal Will from me?"

"Oh, yes," Columba said. "Stop it!" Her hands closed into fists, with the thumb tips protruding between middle and ring fingers. She sang softly and whirled the fists in front of her in a complicated pattern. Maya could almost see what she was sketching in the air, but not quite. Columba drew in a ragged breath. "Get out!"

"How long does the tell-all part last?" Dr. Porta asked.

"An hour or two. I mean it! Get out of here!"

Dr. Porta flung her zippered pouches into her satchel, packed the camera a little more carefully, and grabbed the potion bowl. "You got it." She brushed past Sarutha on her way out of the apartment.

"Columba, what have you been up to?" Sarutha asked, her soft, ancient face creased with frown.

"Security things," said Columba.

"Have you been doing things to Maya?"

"Sure," said Columba. "You knew I would. That's why you sent her here. Only necessary things, though. Have you seen the Rimi friend, Sarutha?"

"Not directly."

"Huge. Bigger than you imagine. And—later," she said, with a shrug. "I don't want to converse with anyone right now."

Maya shouldered her backpack. She went to the kitchen threshold and studied the orchids in the front room. They looked innocent. Of course, they would.

"Damn," said Columba. "I shouldn't be chasing you off. I have to keep watch on you, and I need to find out more about you. It's my job. Just don't ask me any more questions, okay?"

"I'm not making any promises," Maya said. Sarutha took her hand and led her toward the apartment door.

"Are you as diabolical as that makes you sound?" Columba asked, following them.

"Probably not," said Maya.

"Is your name Turnip Khachaturian?"

"What are you talking about?"

"Why doesn't the tell-all tea work on you?" Columba asked. "You drank more of it than I did."

"I'd rather not say," said Maya.

"*Kiri alamaka,*" Columba muttered. "Well," she said. "I suppose you're in safe hands for now, and I can stop watching you."

# EIGHTEEN

Maya followed Sarutha up two sets of stairs to the third floor. Another set of stairs led higher in the building. Maya had studied it from outside and was pretty sure the building had five above-ground stories, but she'd never been higher than Sarutha's floor.

Sarutha's apartment was very small, a studio: one room, with a kitchen corner that had a sink, a two-burner hot plate, and a tiny under-the-counter fridge with a piece of red counter above it. The walls were dark, a mosaic of different kinds of polished woods with knotholes like a design in them. For furniture, a round, wooden table stood near the kitchen corner with its own chairs. A big, comfortable couch that doubled as Sarutha's bed sat on piled carpets in dark reds, blues, and browns. Black ironwork shelves around the room supported delicate sword-leafed plants with spidery baby plants dangling from them. There was a bookshelf with curlicues of iron, and several shiny bird cages that looked like the skeletons of dollhouses with the shapes of roofs and windows and multiple stories in them. The doors to the bird cages were always open. Sometimes birds went inside the cages, and sometimes there were no birds. Most of them were wild birds. Sarutha left seeds in the seed containers in the cages, and she tried to leave at least one window open, no matter what the weather. At times her apartment was loud with birdsong.

French doors led out onto a little balcony inset in the side of the building that held more plants, one more bird-cage, and two chairs. Maya headed for the balcony; it was where they always studied together if they were in the apartment instead of in one of the classrooms, unless the outside weather was too fierce or cold.

Maya loved the view of her neighborhood from this height. Sarutha's balcony faced toward Maya's house. She could look down at her own roof, her own chimney, her own backyard, where Sully the golden retriever slept, or ran after squirrels, or played with Peter. The carport was on the far side of the house, so she couldn't see whether Mom's and Dad's cars were parked there, but she could see lights in the windows of the living room, dining room, her room, and Peter's room, if lights were on. She could see the greenway between the two halves of the block, too, with houses to either side. The greenway dead-ended at Janus House, which covered a third of the block and had a few associated structures with it. Maya liked this bird's-eye view of life. She felt safe up here in Sarutha's hidden place.

Sarutha leaned over by the fridge and came up with two cans of grapefruit soda. She brought them out to the balcony and set them on wooden coasters on the little wicker table. Then she sat down, with a fluffing of velvet skirts around her as she lowered herself into the chair.

"Columba wants me to work with her," Maya said after they had opened their sodas and taken the first bubbly sip.

"Do you like her?" Sarutha asked.

"I think so."

"You could do worse."

"I thought you and I were working together."

"Yes, my dear. Of course. I treasure you as a student. But you know you have many teachers here."

It was true; Maya saw one person for language lessons on Monday, a different person for singing class on Wednesday, and yet another person for principles of magic class on Friday. Sarutha was her teacher for more nebulous subjects, like family trees, the history of portals, and the different species who used portals. She was gracious about answering Maya's questions, and she made Maya feel safe.

"Your singing teacher says you don't have musical gifts, Maya."

"What?" Maya touched her throat. She loved to sing, and everybody complimented her voice at home.

"You are a wonderful singer, for a human," Sarutha said. "You understand that we here are something different, yes?"

"Magic," Maya said.

"We have been bred to host magic in our throats, in our bones, in our voices and our hands. We were not sure if the *sissimi* bond would grant you any of that magic. *Sissimi* are from another system. They don't call what they do magic; to them it is science, or life, or just what they do. Portal users all have different ways they believe in the workings of portals, and belief is what makes the portals work. On Earth, we use song and magic. Your *sissimi* gives you many powers, but they are not like our powers; so it is time you focused on things you can excel at."

"So my classes—I could tell what I was trying didn't work," Maya said in a small voice. She was there with all those five- and six-year-olds, trying to raise sparks, or change airflow, or wake a glyph written on a slate, and the Littles were getting things to work, but Maya never could manage to affect anything, even though her teacher said she was doing everything right.

"It is not that you lack skill," Sarutha said. "It is that it is just not in you."

*It might be in* me, Rimi thought. *I will acquire all the powers I see and then we'll be able to do everything they can.*

*Rimi,* Maya thought, in the midst of despair. She had never even thought of making her own magic, not seriously—outside the stories Stephanie had made up about both of them being magical changelings whose abilities would manifest any day now—until she started taking the basic classes at Janus House. She had learned to watch Gwenda's small motions, Benjamin's hands, Rowan's eyes, guessing which natural forces they might be pushing or shifting. They tried not to do any of it outside the house, but they practiced every day, and some slippage happened.

*Really, Maya. I am that thing in which many worlds meet; so I know from Vati and Kita. In us, you and I meet, but may-be I can meet others long enough to acquire—*

Maya rubbed her eyes, smiling, and thought, *Having you is enough.*

Rimi pressed her cheek gently. *Well, all right, for now. I am always looking, though. I will find us powers.*

"The particular skills we have, you will not be able to acquire," Sarutha said. "It's possible you could drop singing and magic principles classes—"

"Even if I can't do things, maybe I can learn about them, so I know what you guys are doing," Maya said.

"If you feel that way, then of course, please continue to study. If you are frustrated by the classes, know that you can give them up. We could design other training for you that would prove more useful. Meanwhile, though, you and Rimi are developing these other skills that could be very, very valuable to us. Columba could give you a new curriculum suited specifically to your skills and potential." Sarutha paused and looked over the neighborhood. Dusk was coming, and a cool wind was chasing leaves off the trees. Maya hunched her shoulders, and Rimi warmed around her, stopping the wind from chilling her.

*You are the best magic,* Maya thought.

*I know,* Rimi thought, with the creamy feel and lemon meringue taste of her smile.

"Meanwhile, about the homework I gave you," Sarutha said.

Maya unzipped her pack and pulled out the manila envelope. She opened it, then tilted it to shake the piece of folded material out. It sizzled against her hands, though, and she dropped it. "Ouch!"

*Not nice!* Rimi picked up the material and shook it out. It was heavy dark canvas, with a picture embroidered on it in thick colored thread. It showed three people close together. The people were not human. They had wings hunched on their backs, and their hair was like heavy vines that reached the ground, though some of it curled and hung around their bodies as though it were tentacles. They posed as formally as people in Egyptian tomb paintings. Two had wing-hands extended, their arms bent with one hand facing up and the other down, and the third person had wing-hands bunched tight, hands folded beneath his chin, head bent forward.

*Krithi*, Rimi thought.

"Krithi," Maya said at the same time, her voice tight. She flexed her hands, which were red and painful. White blisters puffed up through the reddened skin. Pain made tears spill from Maya's eyes.

"Did the picture hurt you? I'm so sorry," Sarutha said.

She looked at the picture hanging in the air, then leaned over Maya's hands. "Let me help you."

Maya held her hands out, and Sarutha crooned and waved her hands above them. The red and the pain faded, and the blisters sank away.

"Thank you," Maya said. "Why would it do that?"

"I don't know," Sarutha said. "I've touched it and nothing happened. I never expected it to hurt you. Rimi, can you discover anything about it?"

*I will* sisti *it,* Rimi thought.

*I've heard you say that before,* Maya thought. *What does that mean?*

*It is all the senses I can use without touching something, though I am already touching this, but not with my* fenshu, *and it is—it is strange. There are* slurzies *in it, little things that are almost alive.* Rimi laid the picture on the balcony floor. *There. Not touching it any longer, and the* slurzies *are quiet now. Now I* sisti.

Maya felt Rimi exploring the picture. Rimi studied it and saw an overlay of colored light that formed a symbol. The lines were light green except where they crossed each other, and there they glowed red. They looked woven, and then there were some doodly parts. Maya got out her sketchbook and drew the symbol, then sketched a quick copy of the Krithi images.

Rimi shifted and looked again, and this time Maya sensed handprints on the cloth, mostly around the edges. She sensed them as some kind of blurring, with a sort of scent or personal marker attached. Some of the blurs smelled familiar to Rimi—Sarutha's touch was there, Columba's, Harper's. Others, under the Janus House people prints, smelled alien to Maya.

Rimi moved closer, drawing in the scents. *Oh, I remember.*

*Krithi*, Rimi thought. Maya felt a prickling of Rimi's sadness. *Is that the right word? It might not be, but I didn't know words then. I remember the people. I don't remember them very well, because it was before I had frames for think-ing. I remember being torn from the mother plant, and finding my friend. I wasn't quite ready for that, not quite ripe, but old enough to survive it. Then my friend and I were taken elsewhere, and that hurt as though I burned with fire. The portal! Worse pain than being ripped from the mother plant. If I hadn't had my friend to nest against, I would have died.*

*Then we came to another place that was much hotter and drier. Friend and I went into the baths there and floated in warmth and comfort, and there were tastes like none I've found here, and the rush of his feelings, and so much new around me, and other people's touches, and tests and probes, though I only know that now, not then. Then it was just pushing, poking, things coming into Friend and taking bits out. Some of the tastes and feelings I loved. I remember—there was a friendnet there, too, two more of me and their friends. We weren't allowed to touch, but I could still sense their nearness. I learned Bikos's name, and his feelings. We learned to join—*

Rimi broke off. Maya felt fluttering against her skin, and then a tightening as Rimi wrapped around her. *You're mine*, Rimi thought.

*Yes*, thought Maya.

*Part of me is still Bikos. As part of you is still Stephanie.*

Maya wasn't as sure about this, but she thought, *Yes.*

Rimi was still. She leaned into the cloth again, collecting smells/senses/heat/magic traces. *One of the ones who touched this, it was someone Bikos knew. There were three important people who stayed with him—the guardian one, the mother one, and the smooth-everything one. These memories are so fuzzed to me, though. I was never under Bikos's skin the way I was with you. I didn't get a chance to be inside his senses all the way, and my own senses were babies then, not* very sharp. I caught the big feelings, but not the little details. One of these touches on the cloth, though, it is from someone we knew.

"Maya? Rimi?" asked Sarutha.

"Where did this come from? One of the people who touched it was someone who knew Bikos."

Sarutha drew in a sharp breath, a hiss over her lips. "One of Columba's agents was doing an energy scan. Routine. He saw a knot of strange energy in a park a little north of town, and when he went to investigate, he found this, and scorch marks on the ground. It's energy we haven't seen before. We, too, suspected Krithi, but we weren't sure, despite the artwork. I need to report this to Harper." She stood up. "Is there anything else you can tell me?"

Rimi pressed herself against the cloth. Flurries of spitting sparks rushed up at her, and she snapped back. *It's still alive, and it's watching,* she thought. *I shouldn't have touched it. Now it knows I'm here.*

# NINETEEN

"Oh, no," Maya said.

"Tell me," said Sarutha.

Maya stood up and held out her hands. She tugged on Rimi, though she didn't know how she was doing it. She pulled Rimi to her, gathered in her scarves and waves and wings, her flows and flowers, pressed them all together and hugged her tight. Rimi clung to her. For the first time, Maya had a sense that Rimi had weight—not a lot of weight, but substance, mass, dimension. She had seen Rimi as large when Dr. Porta's visibility potion kicked in, but she had still been thinking of Rimi in shadow terms.

"Maya? Rimi?" Sarutha said.

"Rimi says the cloth is alive, and now it knows we're here."

"*Kiri alamaka*," Sarutha muttered. "Stand back."

Maya boosted Rimi and backed off the balcony and into Sarutha's apartment.

Sarutha rubbed her hands together and flexed her fingers, rubbed the balls of her thumbs across her fingertips. She sang three notes, then made some very fast finger motions while singing a song with lots of short notes that bounced up and down. Maya could almost see an outline of the song, with lots of peaks and valleys, and black and red tints. Sarutha crossed her index and middle fingers one over another and pointed toward the cloth, then sang something strong, loud, and fast.

Rimi stirred against Maya's shoulder. *I* sisti *it*, she said. *She sends stop power at the cloth. Now it wraps around it, and nothing can get out.*

Sarutha snapped her fingers, stood with one finger on her chin, then closed her first two fingers over her thumbs on both hands and sang something else, waving her fists at the cloth. She snapped her hands open, and Rimi thought, *A second layer of nothing-gets-out. Good. Good.* Rimi stopped drooping and lifted her own weight off of Maya, living in air again the way she always had, a buoyant being.

"That should do it," Sarutha said. She went to her power picture, an ugly picture of a big-eyed kitten, and tapped it to open communications. She spoke with someone at the other end in Kerlinqua. The only word Maya recognized was *dirty*.

The picture answered her. They had a short exchange, and then Sarutha nodded and turned away. "Columba will send a containment team up, and we'll isolate it so it can't send any more information out. Rimi, do you know whether it was sending bulletins earlier?"

*I think it only woke up when I touched it with my* fenshu. *Before that it was stupid and dead.*

*It burned me,* Maya thought.

*I think it was just kicking while it was asleep. It didn't mean it.*

Maya looked at her healed hands and thought how awful it would have been if Sarutha hadn't helped her. If she couldn't hold a pencil to draw, she was pretty sure she'd go crazy.

*If your hand ever hurts that much again, I'll make you a hand,* Rimi thought.

Maya blinked. *Love you,* she thought.

"Rimi? Maya?" Sarutha said.

"Rimi thinks it wasn't awake until she touched it, and you jumped right on it," Maya said.

"*Aleyma*," Sarutha said. "Thank goodness, and badness, and every ness between. Columba will alert the watchers to track any other obtrusive energy, especially if it moves our direction. They would be doing that anyway, but sometimes it helps to remind them."

Sarutha came close and laid her hand on Maya's shoulder. She looked deep into Maya's eyes. "Think about this, my dearest one. A strange and scary thing happened, but still, before and after and around it, you and Rimi were exploring, learning, and telling me what you discovered. This is exactly the sort of thing Columba does. She may be your natural workmate."

"But Namdi, I want to be an artist. I don't see how that fits in with security."

"You drew us a picture of the person we were to search for, when Bikos was lost. You've showed us visions of the Krithi home planet we have not seen before. Your art informs us, and it is beautiful, too. Your skill works with this job very well."

"But that's—" Maya thought of the graphic novels she'd

imagined drawing. She and Steph had had a master plan, writer and illustrator team. They had ideas for several fantasy series. Maya had cut that plan loose when Stephanie died. It had been creeping back into her mind recently, small and secret, only its edges visible.

*We can do both*, Rimi thought.

"No decisions are necessary now," Sarutha said. "Take your time thinking about it. Just know in the meantime that we very much appreciate your help and skill." Sarutha patted her shoulder. "Time's up for today, my dear. I'll see you Friday."

Maya glanced at her watch. Five minutes to five. "Okay," she said. "Thanks, Namdi."

# TWENTY

"Do you know what costume you're going to wear yet?" Helen asked Maya Thursday morning before language arts class started.

"I don't even know what ghost to write my story about," Maya said. "Did you decide whether to trick-or-treat?"

"I think I'll go," said Helen.

"Yeah, why not? Disguise yourself, meet the neighbors, get free candy. Hey, where do you live? Do you want to come with me?"

Helen looked at her, considering. Maya got that judged-and-dismissed feeling. She hated it. That was one thing she had enjoyed about being adopted by Janus House—they couldn't dismiss her once she and Rimi bonded. They had to figure out how to make the best of her being one of them. Sure, they judged, but they couldn't vote her off the island.

"Maybe you already have plans with your other friends," Maya said.

"Don't you have plans with yours?" Helen asked softly as Ms. Caras rushed in and took her place behind the teacher's desk.

"We haven't talked about it much, but I think I'm going to convince Gwenda to come with me." Maya glanced at Travis, on her other side. He was doing his best sleep-imitation-or-reality, body sagging in total relaxation, head lolled to one side, mouth half open, soft snores coming out. "Travis is going to be handing out candy, so he can't come. That's about as far as I've gotten."

"Don't you have siblings? You talked about them that first day when we were discussing our summers."

"Yeah, a younger brother. My sister's seventeen. She's too cool to go out."

The bell rang, leaving Maya with the unsettled sensation of a conversation only half finished. Helen hadn't answered the question about whether she'd join Maya trick-or-treating.

*Whatever you do, whoever you are, I'll be with you,* Rimi thought.

*Thanks, Rimi.*

"All right, class," said Ms. Caras. "Ghost stories are due tomorrow. Everybody already wrote a suspenseful opening, starting with a sound in the house. You can use that as your story start, or start over, but remember to keep it scary. I hope you've all settled on who your ghost is and whom your ghost is haunting. The rest of the story should write itself. I'll give you some writing time now. If questions come up, raise your hand and I'll come and talk to you. Anything before we start?"

One of the other kids raised a hand. "I found a list of ghost rules at a site online," he said, "and I made copies." He waved a handful of papers.

"Wonderful, Reuben," said Ms. Caras. "Let's pass those out and take a look at them. Remember, there are a lot of different versions of ghosts, so if you don't like these rules, you can find others, or make some up. This could give you a starting point, though."

The rules were from a TV show about a woman who could talk to ghosts. Maya read down through them, mentally checking whether she believed them. Some of them seemed like other ghost rules she'd heard—ghosts could create cold spots, ghosts could go through things. Some of the rules were strange. Some seemed made up to make the show work. Most of them made Maya think of stories. If only Stephanie could see the list, she'd be off and running with a story in a second.

Helen flipped through the pages and then nudged Maya. "Find your ghost yet?" she whispered.

Maya shook her head. "Nope."

"Here's an idea for you. Twin ghosts."

Twin ghosts! Maya thought about it and liked it. "How did they die?" she whispered.

"Their mother locked them in the car and pushed it into a lake."

"Ewww!"

"That really happened," Helen whispered. "Well, not the ghost part, and not the twin part, but a mother locked her kids in the car and drowned them.

"Why aren't you using that one?"

"I don't believe in ghosts. But I've already decided to write something else. You can use that one."

"Okay," said Maya. "What are you writing?"

Helen folded the ghost rules and tucked them into her

messenger bag. "A girl and her brother's ghost," she whispered.

Maya thought about Peter as a ghost. He probably knew all the ghost rules from the books he had been reading, so he'd know how to be a good ghost. But—no, she didn't want to think about Peter dead.

"Reuben, thanks again for sharing this interesting information," Ms. Caras said. "Here's the way some people divide up ghosts." She went to the white board and wrote, "Dead People," "Recorded Events," "Poltergeists," and "Fake Ghosts."

Ms. Caras said, "Some people think ghosts are dead people who can talk and think and act as though they were alive." She tapped the words "Dead People."

"Other people think there's kind of a ghost recording of a traumatic event that happened in a particular place that replays. Like if someone was murdered in the bedroom, you might see that murder replayed once a night." She tapped "Recorded Events." "In that case, there's nobody there, really, it's just a replay. Some kind of psychic energy makes an imprint on a place, and you hear someone singing the same song in the hallway every night, or footsteps going down the staircase to the basement every time it rains. It can be spooky, but you can get used to it, and it won't hurt you."

She tapped the next label. "The third kind of ghost is a poltergeist, or noisy ghost, something that throws things, breaks things, turns faucets or electronics on and off, or generally makes mischief. These might be ghosts or dead people, but a lot of people think this energy comes from troubled teenagers." She looked at each student in turn. "You are all probably lovely people for whom everything goes right—no poltergeists in this class. But maybe you know somebody weird things happen around."

Helen looked sideways at Maya. Maya smiled and looked sideways at someone else.

*I could move something right now*, Rimi thought. The eraser on the ledge below the white board twitched.

*I don't think that's a good idea*, Maya thought. *We're supposed to be keeping our own secrets.*

Salla. *You're probably right.* The eraser settled. *Though how would they know it's* our *secret?*

"And finally," said Ms. Caras, "Fake Ghosts. Sometimes these are tricks people set up to fool other people, like séances where fake mediums pretend to communicate with the dead. Other times it's all in a person's head: they think they're seeing and hearing things they aren't."

She leaned against the whiteboard and smiled at the class. "You can use any of these ideas, or others if you have them. Now, everyone, start your storytelling."

Maya wrote her name and the class and date at the top of a piece of paper, then sat with the tip of her pencil on the top line where she would put a title.

*Let me*, Rimi thought, gently tugging at the pencil. Maya let go of it but kept her hand loosely cupped around it, moving her hand as the pencil moved. When it stopped, she had to move her hand to see what Rimi had written.

The handwriting was neater than Maya's, but looked enough like it to pass for Maya being extra neat. "What the Water Taught Us," it said.

*Eww*, Maya thought. *Good one*. Maya drew twin girls, about five, pigtails sprouting from both sides of each head. Instead of eyes, they had dark pits. One smiled, and the other had a blank expression. Mostly, she thought, they were probably mad at their mother. She started the story.

When the bell rang at the end of the period, she looked up, surprised. She'd written four pages, complete with illustrations, and was at the part where the mother was going insane because of the twins' haunting.

"Finish up and turn them in tomorrow. Good luck,"

said Ms. Caras as everybody rose and clattered and collected their things and made for the door.

*Maybe I* can *tell a story*, Maya thought. *Maybe that's how
Steph can haunt me. Help me come up with stories. Thank
you, Steph.*

# TWENTY-ONE

Thursday afternoon, Maya had a piano lesson with the music teacher from the elementary school where Maya's mother worked. Ms. Barge was one of Maya's mother's best friends at the new school. She lived a block from the Andersens. Maya had taken lessons from her mother in Idaho, but she liked the change in teachers, even though her mother still encouraged her to practice every day. That was just the way it had always been.

On the way to Ms. Barge's house, Maya stopped at Penny's Mini-Mart for a soda. The store was small, dark, and cool, on a corner not far from her house. She and Peter had gone there first thing when they moved into Spring House to check out the candy selection, which was minimal. The clerks watched them all the time they were in the store, just waiting for them to shoplift, and sometimes that made Maya so mad she went three blocks to the supermarket instead, but today she didn't have time.

She was staring through the cooler's glass doors at her choices when Sybil Katsaros edged up beside her. "Hey," she said.

"Hey," said Maya. At last, they had said something to each other. So far, so good.

*What is this?* Rimi asked. Pattishaw! *This close, I can feel—this is, there's a feel that—who—*

"We should talk," said Sibyl.

Rimi thought, *The scarf. The scarf. It is—from the nursery—one of my sibs.*

*Sibyl has a* sissimi? Maya asked. *Sibyl? OMG.*

*I* sisti *it. Sib!* Rimi reached for Sibyl and her *sissimi,* and then shock sizzled through her and into Maya. Maya staggered and grabbed the chrome handle to the cold case; it was all that held her up as her insides buzzed and jolted. Her legs shook, and her muscles felt like jelly. All Rimi's extensions flexed and flopped wildly around her, brushing against Maya and bumping glass, shelving, floor, every direction but toward Sibyl. Maya gasped and gripped the handle and struggled to find her feet. Sweat beaded on her forehead.

*Rimi!* she thought. *Rimi! Are you okay?*

Ssssizzura! Sizz. Sizz. *Oh, that was bad. Oh! I'm—I'm—I'll reintegrate.* Rimi pulled in close around Maya, wrapped her up in Rimi-stuff, loaned her muscle and stiffening so she could stand up straight. Maya swiped her forehead with the back of her hand, which came away wet. Her stomach jumped, then settled.

"Sorry," said Sibyl. Her glasses gleamed. "We weren't expecting you to try anything like that."

"Try anything?" Maya felt as though she'd just been run over by a roughshod windstorm. "I didn't try anything,"

"Sure you did. Yiliss doesn't attack unprovoked."

"Yiliss," Maya repeated. "Attack." Yes, she had been attacked. *Oh, Rimi!*

"You know what I'm talking about. A *sissimi.* You got one, too, right? But I never saw you in the sand pits."

"The sand pits," Maya whispered.

"Are you going to go on playing dumb and repeat everything I say, or can we have some kind of a conversation here?"

Maya shuddered and pulled herself up straight. She

stroked her hand across the invisible Rimi wrapping around her. "I'm not playing dumb," she said. "I am dumb. I don't understand anything you're talking about."

"You can do better than that. You can start by explaining why you ditched the Methry, why you're hanging out with those creepy Janus kids and that loser Travis, why I never saw you in the sand pits—"

"What's Methry?" Maya asked.

"Methry," Sibyl said, waving her hand as though she could make Maya understand by nudging the air near her head. "The Kalithri trainers."

"I still don't know what you're talking about," Maya said.

Sibyl frowned at her. "This ignorance act is getting *so* old!"

"It's not an act," Maya said. *Rimi, I'm so sorry. I know we need to find out more about your brother, but I'm scared of him now. That hurt.*

*I echo your apprehensions. I*—Rimi did something that tightened across Maya's skin. *I close myself to him. I don't want to accept that energy again. I will not fuse. I don't want him to hurt you, Mayamela! I need to access everything I've learned about protection from Kita and Vati. I can make our* shield bubble next time he attacks if I have to. *I will set myself to do that.*

"God, you are too stupid to live!" Sibyl cried, anguish in her tone.

"Great," said Maya. "On that note, I'm leaving." Maya opened the cold case and pulled out a can of Dr Pepper. She pressed the chilled can to her forehead. The cold helped.

She glanced sideways at Sibyl. She had thought when she met another *sissimi* pair it would be a good thing. Her contacts with Ara-Kita and Kachik-Vati had convinced her it was all good, but Sibyl—

They had found one of the missing *sissimi*. She needed to let the Janus House people know.

Ms. Barge would be expecting her in a few minutes.

She was still shaken. She tightened her pack straps and headed for the front of the store. Sibyl had told Maya her secret, but Maya wasn't prepared to deal with it. She needed to talk to Sarutha even more than she needed a piano lesson.

*Yiliss,* thought Rimi. *His name wasn't Yiliss when I knew him through the mothernet. He didn't feel like—but he tastes—he is* sissimi, *he is my sibling, we are fruit of the same vine, but he is no longer the one I knew.*

*Are you the one he knew?* Maya asked.

*Oh. No,* Rimi thought. *No. I am made of me and you and Bikos. I am part Ara-Kita and Kachik-Vati. I have hatched and intermixed and integrated, and all that has changed me. This one used to be near me on the vine when we were all unformed and intermixed, back home. A brother-self, a close love. When we were in the desert place, when Bikos and I were learning each other and bonding, I knew this brother, too, and I knew that Sibyl, but I was a seed, and I did not perceive her as I do now.*

*Now this one, the one now called Yiliss, is made of Sibyl and some other things that taste like metal and oil, some shaping that came from others not bonded to him. As though someone has trimmed his roots and shoots, cut off pieces of him.*

Sibyl said, "I'm doing this all wrong. I'm not supposed to insult you. I want to make friends with you."

"Like that's going to happen," Maya said. "All you've done so far is shock me silly and call me names."

"Wait," Sibyl said. "Wait. Okay, so I didn't get the diplomat training, okay?"

Maya paused. "No lie."

"We're special. We're different. But we're more like each other than anybody else, except for the Hasible, and he's not really like us, either. He's all gray and he gets mad a lot.

And anyway, the Methry sent him to Shostrunim, so even if I wanted to talk to him, I couldn't. But you and me—we should be able to relate. I'm so lonely," Sibyl said. She reached for Maya's arm.

Maya jerked back. "I don't want another shock," she said.

Sibyl held up her hands, palms front. "Okay, okay. Yiliss didn't—I didn't mean to—I wasn't going to—please. Give me a minute to figure this out."

"Take all the time you want." Maya headed to the cash register.

"You okay?" said the skinny, pimply college kid clerk waiting there. He was new. "I saw you in the mirror. Looked like you spazzed out. Did you have a fit?"

"I guess I did," Maya said. She wondered why he hadn't come to help her.

"You kind of got it back together," he said, answering her unasked question, "and then it looked like you were just talking to that girl, so I figured you were okay. If you need help, give a yell, okay?"

Maya blew out a breath. So he might have helped her, if he had been able to figure out she needed it. "Yeah. Thanks." She handed him money and he gave her change.

Maya glanced at Sibyl over her shoulder. The other girl was lost in thought, but she looked up. Maya tightened her lips and pushed out of the store. Janus House or Ms. Barge's? Sarutha should be first, but Maya needed to let her piano teacher know she had to skip. She went to the phone booth, looked up Ms. Barge in the phone book, and called her on the cell phone. "Ms. Barge, something's come up, and I can't make it to my lesson."

"Are you all right?" asked Ms. Barge.

"Feeling a little rocky," Maya said. "I'm going to check with the doctor next door. I'm sorry I didn't have time to give you better notice."

"That's all right this time, Maya. Don't make a habit of it. Take care of yourself."

"Thanks, Ms. Barge." Maya closed her flip phone. When she turned around, Sibyl was standing outside the phone booth staring in at her.

Maya edged the door open. "What?"

"Can we start over?"

Maya took a deep breath and let it out. "Okay. Hi. You have a *sissimi*. His name is Yiliss. I understand that part."

Sibyl stroked her golden scarf. "This is Yiliss."

Maya nodded.

"What's yours named?"

*Do we tell her? I* so *don't feel safe here,* Maya thought.

*My name. I don't think it can hurt me. Let's try.*

"Mine is named Rimi," Maya said.

Sibyl unscrewed the cap on her root beer, and it fizzed up and ran over her hand, splattering the front of her red dress. "Shee-oot!" she cried, and then the golden scarf around her neck unwound itself, reached down its fringed and tasseled ends, and sucked the root beer right out of the fabric. "Thanks," Sibyl muttered, and held her wet hand up to the scarf, which wrapped around it. The scarf thrust a tassel into the root beer bottle, too. When it retreated, Sibyl's hand was clean and dry, and half the root beer was gone.

"You are such a pig, Yiliss!" Sibyl said, but she laughed.

"Yiliss drinks root beer?" asked Maya.

"He loves sweets," said Sibyl. "Usually I have to use half my allowance to buy him treats. It's the only way I can stop him from shoplifting."

"Gosh. Rimi eats a lot of weird stuff, but I don't have to feed her candy," said Maya. "Can you taste what Yiliss is eating?"

"Huh?" said Sibyl. "No. Are you saying you can taste what yours eats? That is *so* weird."

"Not all the time," Maya said, "but sometimes." She shuddered. "Rimi eats garbage."

"Oh, no!"

They stared at each other, their eyes wide. Then, suddenly, they were muffling giggles, then laughing out loud.

When Sibyl caught her breath, she asked, "So what does yours look like? Is it your hoodie? I thought probably not, because you have three different hoodies. Unless yours can change color. Yiliss can do a couple other colors, but he always looks kind of the same."

"Mine's—" *Rimi, I don't want her to know you're my shadow! I don't want her to know anything important!*

*That's all right,* Rimi thought. She poured part of herself into Maya's front hoodie pocket. *I'll be like hers.*

Maya reached into her pocket and pulled out a bunched-up scarf, the yarn soft as chick feathers, woven with holes in it. It was much bigger when she spread it out than she would have thought possible. It was longer than it was wide, but it was almost as big as a tablecloth, though fine as gossamer. Color shimmered across it, pale pink and yellow, green and blue, with threads of gold and silver glinting in it. She spread it wide, flapped it, then rolled it thin and tucked it back into her pocket.

"Wow," Sibyl said. She frowned. "Pretty," she said, her tone gruff.

"Yeah," said Maya, "but I'm not really a scarf person, so it's kind of—I keep her in my pocket." Maya patted the small part of Rimi that was the scarf, feeling the larger part still wrapping her round.

"So where were you on Thrixa? You didn't train with us. Was there a second program somewhere else?" Sibyl asked.

Maya just looked at Sibyl, then away.

"Come on. You don't have to keep secrets anymore, not from me, anyway. You're like me. You must have been involved in a different egg collection mission, though, because I trained with the other two who grabbed eggs when I did. Actually, there were five of us, but two got caught. Where did you train? Just tell me, all right?"

Maya stopped on the sidewalk and turned to Sibyl.

"Okay," she said. "I'll tell you. I was never on Krithi, or Thrixa, or whatever it's called. I wasn't part of any program. I don't understand any of those weird words you're using, because I'm from Earth, and I've lived here all my life. Okay?"

"No!" said Sibyl. "That makes no sense at all!"

"Did you know someone named Bikos Serani?"

"Bikos! *Sivertha*, of course! He was the other successful one besides the Hasible, and I thought he came to Earth, too, but I didn't see him, even though we were both supposed to be going to the same school." Sibyl frowned. "I'm supposed to show how well I can survive on Earth without help, and Bikos was supposed to do that, too, until we're ready for the next part of our mission. The Methry said we could talk to each other in school if we acted like strangers the first time we met. I wanted to see him again . . . but he wasn't here." She looked away from Maya, toward the houses across the street.

# TWENTY-TWO

"Are you originally from Earth?" Maya asked.

"Sure," said Sibyl. "I lived here until I was seven, and then Gaelli found me, and—well, wait. What about Bikos? What can you tell me?"

"He was from someplace else. Not Earth. You knew that, right? He got a *sissimi* egg. The Krithi put him on Earth, and he couldn't eat the food or breathe the air very well. He got really sick, and then he asked me to take care of the egg for him. Like, randomly. And then he—he died."

Sibyl pulled in a hissing breath. "Oh. Oh, no. Oh."

Maya sighed. "Yeah. It was sad. . . . So I took care of the *sissimi*, and she hatched, and we're a pair, but I didn't have any training. I don't speak whatever language you keep talking to me in, and I don't know your Golly-guy." Maya stroked her Rimi-scarf. "Rimi was just trying to find out who you were and whether we could be friends when Yiliss attacked us."

Sibyl's mouth actually dropped open, and she stared at Maya. Then she shook her head like someone trying to wake up. "Whoa. Rewind and start over. I need to reboot my brain. Okay. I'm sorry I gave you such a hard time." She muttered "Whoa!" a few more times.

Maya walked toward home and Janus House. Sibyl, still staring at distance, kept up with her. "So anyway," Maya said after she'd sucked down some Dr Pepper and given Sibyl time to stop "whoa"ing, "I don't know from Methry or Kalithri or any of that stuff."

"Okay. I get that. How the heck did you manage to hatch and bond without any training?"

Maya drank Dr Pepper. "Lucky, I guess."

"That's amazing," Sibyl said.

They had reached Maya's block, the block with Janus House on it. Maya stared across the street at Janus House. Sibyl followed her gaze.

"Is that—what is that place?" she asked.

"Janus House," Maya said. It was public knowledge.

"Where those weirdo kids come from. The ones you're always hanging out with."

Maya checked for traffic and headed across the street. Sibyl walked with her. "Yeah. I live next door," she said, pointing to her own house. Maya wasn't sure she wanted Sibyl to come inside, but she didn't know where else to go. "So we got to know them."

Sarutha was sitting on the Janus House porch with her backstrap loom, watching them. Maya didn't wave, and Sarutha didn't, either.

*I don't think we'd better tell Sibyl and Yiliss anything more about Janus House than we can help*, Maya thought.

*That layer of secrets we keep to ourselves*, Rimi thought. *And many others. I do not trust them.*

"'We'?" Sibyl repeated.

"My family." Not exactly a secret, either. Maya glanced at her Dr Pepper and Sibyl's root beer. They both had drinks, but as the hostess, she felt she should offer something. "Want some tea or something?"

"Sure, I guess," said Sibyl.

Maya led her into the house through the front door and back to the kitchen.

No one else was home yet. Maya shrugged out of her pack and put the kettle on, got down two mugs. "Cocoa? Tea? Instant coffee?"

"Cocoa," Sibyl said.

"Have a seat." Maya gestured toward the kitchen table, and Sibyl sat. "Where do you live?" Maya got cocoa packets from the cupboard and poured them into the mugs. "I never found out where Bikos lived. I think maybe he was living in the park."

"I live with a family that thinks I'm an exchange student from Canada. I'm not sure how Gaelli set that up."

"Who's Gaelli?" Maya asked.

"He's—we had these people who took care of us on Thrixa, and Gaelli is the one who protected us and trained us and brought us here. He left me with this family. They're kind of nice, but they're kind of afraid of me, too. Yiliss did a couple of strange things soon after he hatched that I forgot Earth people wouldn't understand. Now they think Canadians are really weird and a little scary." Sibyl shrugged. "I'm learning survival skills all the time. So far I'm surviving okay."

"The Krithi just dropped you and Bikos here and told you to make it on your own?"

Sibyl winced again. "Please don't call them that!"

"What? Krithi? What's wrong with Krithi?"

"Krithi is the drone people, the worker class that's too low to converse with. They have no brains. It's an insult. The people who took care of me, Bikos, and the Hasible were Methry, special trainers, members of the Kalithri, which is the teaching and government class."

"Okay," Maya said and shrugged again. "What do they call their planet, then?"

"Thrixa," Sibyl said.

"Okay. The Thrixa people just dropped you and your egg here? And Bikos and Rimi's egg?" The kettle whistled, and Maya poured hot water into the cocoa mugs and handed one, with a spoon, to Sibyl.

Sibyl stirred, staring down into her mug. Then she glanced up at Maya. "Gaelli arranged for me to have that host family. I thought Bikos had a host family, too, but I got dropped off first, so I didn't see where he went. And we have help lines," Sibyl said. She frowned and drummed her hands on the table. "We can call the Methry if we're in total distress. I don't get why Bikos didn't do that."

Maya sat down, her warm mug gripped between her hands. The spoon jangled as she set the mug on the table.

She stirred the lumpy powder into the hot water. The scent of chocolate drifted up. *Rimi, you were there. Do you remember anything about this?*

*I remember we had guardians when we were still in the hot place. I couldn't count then, but when I think now, I remember three beings were most concerned with us, making sure we got enough to eat, enough rest, that we were comfortable. Also, they made Bikos work and learn and be busy with things I couldn't understand.*

*When Bikos was so sick, right before he gave you to me, did he think about calling these guardians?* Maya wondered.

Rimi was quiet. Finally she said, *He had many many thoughts. He was very sick. And he was confused. We were not inside each other's minds the way you and I can be; we had bonded, but it was not the complete bond you and I share. What I remember about it: before he got really sick, he met someone and talked to them. It wasn't one of the Krithi, but it was someone who didn't feel local either. Someone who confused him. Many of Bikos's feelings shifted after this encounter. He had been thinking he would find help from the Krithi, or Thrixa, and then that avenue was cut off. The new person made everything inside him shift. Then he just wanted to find someone with* chikuvny *who was not Krithi. He was thinking about saving me, and then I was so sick I couldn't really think, either, though I was trying to save him, but I couldn't do anything inside the seed. I don't remember that part very well, except we were both in such distress.* Rimi's self flushed with warmth, and she hugged Maya a little tighter. *Then we found you, Mayamela.*

*I am so glad,* Maya thought, and then said to Sibyl, "He was so sick when I met him I didn't get to ask him a lot of questions, and I wouldn't have known enough to ask him that one. It was kind of overwhelming. One day, everything's pretty much normal, except my family just moved here from Idaho, and the next day—space aliens, and *sissimi,* and—" Maya shook her head.

"Whoa," Sibyl said. "I say again, whoa. So you kinda got drafted!"

Maya nodded. She smiled. "Rimi is so great."

Sibyl smiled, too. "I know what you mean." She stirred her cocoa, but before she could drink it, the golden scarf stuck its end into the mug and made slurping sounds. "Hey! Except once in a while! Yiliss, you are so bratty." She gave her scarf a little slap and dragged the drinking end out of the mug, then peeked in. "Whew, there's a little left for me."

Maya laughed. "I can make you another cup. Maybe he wants one of his own."

"I don't want him to get spoiled," Sibyl said.

Yiliss lifted a golden end and waved some fringe at Maya.

"Maybe he needs chocolate," Maya said. She mixed up another mug of cocoa from the still-warm water in the kettle and put it down near Sibyl's first mug. Yiliss dipped an end into it and made big sucking noises. His whole length rippled from one end to the other and back.

Sibyl frowned at Maya. "Well, he says thank you, he needed that, and I say, hey, what did I say about spoiling him?"

"But—" Maya frowned and stared at the floor, trying to work this out. "Okay, sorry," she said. *Was that bad, for me to give him something he wants when she says he can't have it?*

*He said he needed it,* Rimi thought. *You would give me something if I needed it, wouldn't you?*

*If I could. Mostly it seems like you get what you need for yourself.*

*You would give me everything I needed if you could,* Rimi said. *I don't want to fuse with Yiliss. I don't know if I like him anymore, and I don't want him to know our secrets. Although*

*I want to learn how he attacked me, so I can use it if I need to, and learn how to defend against it. I don't like it that she won't give him things he wants.*

*Dad says there's a difference between need and want,* Maya thought.

Rimi was silent. Then she thought, *I'm glad you gave him cocoa.*

*Thanks,* Maya thought.

"Sorry," Sibyl said. "I kind of, well, I'm not the best at talking to people. Still trying to figure that part out."

"How do you get along with your host family?"

Sibyl wrinkled her nose. "Not so well. There's a boy. He's fourteen and creepy. Sometimes it seems like he wants to kiss me, and sometimes he just wants to beat me up. Yiliss discouraged him from that, all right." She smiled, her eyes fixed on distance, and nodded. "Then there's another boy who's nine, and he's pretty much okay, but he snoops, and sometimes he steals. I didn't bring a whole lot of stuff with me from Thrixa. He took my worry stone, though, and I don't think it'll be easy for me to get another. Going through the portals is so expensive. . . ."

"Portals?" Maya said. She didn't trust Sibyl, but Sibyl seemed to trust her. Maya felt a little icky asking Sibyl questions about secret things when she planned to tell the Janus House people everything she learned. Or maybe she wouldn't tell them everything. So many secrets. She couldn't keep track of who knew what.

"That's how we travel from one planet to another. It's not like spaceships. You walk through this weird red light. There's a lot of—well, it hurts, but it goes pretty fast. And somehow you end up somewhere else."

"Weird," Maya said. "And it's expensive?"

"Yeah, it's intense, kind of painful, and it uses a lot of energy, so they save it for special projects."

"You're a special project?"

"Sure. So were Bikos and the Hasible."

"What kind of a project are you?"

Sibyl opened her mouth, closed it, fiddled with Yiliss. "I don't think I'm supposed to talk about it."

"Oh, okay." Better not to push. Maya changed the subject. "You say you're not good at talking to people, but I saw you sitting with Helen and some other kids at lunch the other day. You've been making friends here."

"Not really. Helen is just really nice. She invited me to sit with her and her friends. Awkward. I don't know how to talk to people, I really don't." She sipped the remains of cocoa from her cup. "Like jokes. I totally don't get jokes. Everybody's laughing and I don't get why." She wove her fingers through Yiliss's end fringe, which twined around them, made knots, and untied them. "Back home, we had jokes I could understand."

"Back home on Thrixa?"

"Yeah."

Just then Peter and Mom breezed in through the back-door. They stopped when they discovered Maya and Sibyl.

"Maya? What happened to your piano lesson?" Mom asked.

"I was feeling kind of sick, so I called Ms. Barge and told her I couldn't come," Maya said. "I feel better now. Mom, this is Sibyl. Peter, Sibyl. Sibyl, my mom and my little brother, Peter."

Sibyl nodded. She fiddled with her scarf.

"Hi, Sibyl," Peter said. He had Sully's water bowl in his hand. He went to the sink and poured out the old wa-ter and refilled the bowl, then opened the backdoor and whistled.

Sully came in, smiling a drop-mouthed dog smile, and sniffed at the bowl Peter set down. Then he looked at Sibyl. His black lip lifted in a growl. The sound spun out and out.

Sibyl stood and backed away from him, her hands wrapped in Yiliss.

"Sully!" Peter said. He grabbed Sully's collar and pulled him back out the door, shut the door behind him. "Sorry. He usually doesn't do that."

"Dogs don't like me," Sibyl said. "Anyway, I guess I should be getting home now. Thanks for the cocoa, Maya. See you tomorrow."

"Okay," Maya said. She walked Sibyl out.

On the front porch, Sibyl looked at Maya. "I'm really glad we talked," she said, and then she ran down the steps and on up the sidewalk.

"Maya," her mother said when Maya returned to the kitchen, "I'm glad you're socializing so much at school, but you can't just blow off a piano lesson because you feel like it."

"I'm sorry, Mom. It was kind of an emergency."

"Did this emergency involve throwing up?"

"Almost," Maya said. She remembered the shuddering shakes and terrible off-balance feeling she'd had after Yiliss had shocked her.

Her mother stared at her for a long, uncomfortable minute. "All right," she said at last. "I'm glad you thought to call Ms. Barge."

"Thanks." Maya picked up Sibyl's two mugs and her one, rinsed them, and put them in the dishwasher. She checked the kitchen clock, a black cat with eyes that moved back and forth and a tail that twitched from side to side as the clock ticked. It was a little before four. "I have to run next door."

"Practice first," said her mother.

"Can't I practice after curfew? I will, I promise. An hour instead of half an hour."

Mom sighed, then said, "All right."

Maya grabbed her pack and headed for Janus House.

# TWENTY-THREE

Maya knocked on Columba's door. Columba opened it. "Maya. What is it?"

"I have—I know—I found one of the missing *sissimi.*"

"*Kiri ah!* Come in!"

Maya followed Columba into her kitchen and sat at the table.

*There is someone else here*, Rimi said.

*What? Where?*

*Standing against the wall by the power picture. It's Evren. He is in that* twizzle *mode he stays in when he's at Music Night.*

*Invisible.* Maya stared at the wall with the power picture

on it. She couldn't see even a ripple in the air.

"Tell me," Columba said, sitting down across from her.

"But—Evren—did you know Evren is here?"

Columba heaved a sigh. "Evren is my apprentice, practiced in stealth, and you're not supposed to be able to detect him."

"Rimi can see him."

"Ah. An interesting wrinkle," Columba said. "Evren, uncloak."

Evren faded into sight. "Hi, Maya."

Maya squinted at him. "Stealth, huh? Are you really interested in my sister?"

"I like her."

"But you taking her for a walk—"

"You're right. That's a job. I'm supposed to distract her, maybe give her bad information," he said. He came and sat down at the table, touched Maya's hand. "Don't look at me like that. This is one of the nicer ways we have of handling a problem like Candra, and I really do like her."

"Maya, let's not get off track," said Columba. "You have something to tell us."

Maya studied Evren, deciding whether she wanted to tell him. If he was Columba's apprentice, he probably knew lots of secrets, and she could tell he could keep them, too. Anyway, once she told Columba about Sibyl, Columba would probably tell Great-uncle Harper and a lot of other people. Then what would happen?

"What happens when I tell you this?" she asked.

"We need to get in touch with the Interportal Force. You know the *sissimi* was stolen. It's a criminal matter."

"But he's bonded now. They can't reverse that, can they?"

"I don't think they can." Columba straightened. "You're worried about what will happen to the person and the *sissimi*?"

"Yes," Maya said.

"I respect that." Columba tapped her fingers on the table, one hand, then the other, in a complicated, galloping pattern. She stared at the ceiling, her eyes moving. She lowered her gaze to meet Maya's. "If the situation is stable, we will just take stock of it. No sudden moves. We may need to assign a watcher." She glanced toward Evren. "Evren is our best watcher. In all likelihood, I'll need to bring in someone from the Force, maybe Ara-Kita because of her *sissimi* knowledge, or another *sissimi* bonded pair. This is an interportal matter, Maya. It affects many worlds. It's all of a piece with the Krithi movements of late. Lots of people are worried about this."

*Rimi?*

*You need to tell, because otherwise you'll be sick with worry.*

Maya closed her eyes and let out a breath. Then she sat up straight and faced Columba. "It's another seventh-grade girl, named Sibyl Katsaros. Her *sissimi* is a scarf she wears around her neck. She says the third stolen *sissimi* went to a person called the Hasible, and he was sent somewhere else, to—to Shostrunim? Is that right?"

*Is this right?* Maya asked Rimi.

*Yes.*

"Rimi says it's right. Shostrunim."

"Shostrunim. That's Ara-Kita's home planet," Columba said. "Or Ara's, anyway. Did this girl tell you anything about the Krithi plans for these stolen *sissimi*?"

"She says the word Krithi is an insult," Maya said.

Columba frowned. "It is?"

"She said it means drones or lower-class people. The Krithi call their planet Thrixa, and the teachers and government people are Kalithri, and some other people are Methry. I kind of lost track after a while; she used so many words I didn't know. So I might have some of that backward."

"Interesting cultural notes. Plans, Maya?"

"She said she and Bikos and the Hasible were special projects, but then she clammed up."

"Anything else?"

"The guy who sent her here fixed her up with a foster family. Oh, and her *sissimi* attacked us, and it hurt."

"Are you all right?"

*Rimi, are we all right?*

*All your systems are balanced again, and I have incorporated the force used against me. I will analyze it tonight while you sleep and learn how to use it and defend against it.*

"We're okay, but I had to cancel my piano lesson, and now I'm in trouble with Mom about that."

Columba laughed. Then she coughed. Then she laughed again. "Sorry. I shouldn't laugh about you being in trouble, but it's such little trouble compared to interportal theft and stealth and plans to violate edicts and create mischief."

"I guess," said Maya. "Anyway, I have to get home now and practice the piano."

Columba rose. "Maya, thank you so much for coming to me. Has Sarutha talked to you about apprenticing with me?"

"She mentioned it."

"Please consider it, my dear. I have so many things I could teach you and Rimi, and I'm sure Rimi could teach me a few things."

"All right," Maya said.

"Maya, can you draw us a picture of Sibyl?" Evren asked.

"What? Oh. Sure." She got out her sketchpad and drew several pictures of Sibyl. Sibyl looking belligerent. Sibyl looking lost. Sibyl with her hands buried in her scarf, a tender look on her face. "This is Yiliss, Sibyl's *sissimi*," Maya said, pointing to the scarf in each picture. She tore the pages out of her book and handed them to Evren.

"These are great. You're really good," he said. "Thanks, Maya."

"Sure." She shouldered her pack. "See you tomorrow."

"Yes," said Columba.


As Maya headed out, the door to Benjamin's apartment opened and he emerged. "Hey, Maya. What are you doing here on an off day?"

"Things to report," Maya said. Should she tell him about Sibyl and the *sissimi*? She decided she should. The Janus

House kids were already suspicious of Sibyl. They should know why. Or maybe Columba was supposed to decide who got to know what, but she hadn't told Maya not to tell anyone.

"Sibyl has a *sissimi*," she said.

*"Aya!"*

"But, in other news, do you have plans for Halloween?"

*"Aya!"* he said again, and then, "We don't really do things on Halloween. We strengthen the wards so nobody trick-or-treats here, and that's how we celebrate. I like your pumpkins."

"I'm trying to talk Gwenda into going out with me. You could come, too."

He smiled and shook his head. "What would I dress as? I'm boring."

"You're not boring," Maya said. "You're just secret. The point of Halloween is to let your secret self out. I think you'd make a great pirate."

"A pirate!" He laughed. Then he stopped and looked into the distance. "A pirate," he said, in a different tone of voice. "Yo ho. Which secret self are you going to be?"

Maya bit her lower lip and said, "Rimi is my secret self. We have to figure out how to show that."

"You're going to show it? But—"

"The thing about Halloween is everyone wears a costume, and they all think everyone else is wearing a costume, so we can come as we are, and they'll think it's fake."

"A pirate," Benjamin said. "Does the costume cover me so no one will recognize me?"

"It can if you want it to."

He looked at her, then nodded. "I want it to. I want to go with you, too. Thanks for asking me."

"Well, sure," said Maya. She looked at her watch. "Gotta go home and practice piano."

"But wait. Sibyl has a *sissimi*. That's kind of major."

"Ask Columba about the rest." Maya waved and slipped out the double front doors.

Peter waited through the last ten minutes of Maya's hour of piano practice, even though she was playing the same piece, the Bach Bourrée in E Minor, over and over. It was a tune she had learned the year before, but she liked it better than most of the songs in the new book Ms. Barge had made her buy. While she played it, she could think about things.

When she looked up at the clock and it ticked over to

six P.M., she heaved a sigh and closed the cover over the keyboard, then looked sideways at Peter.

"Halloween," he said.

"Yes."

"Can I go out with you? I don't think Mom and Dad will let me go by myself."

"What are you going to dress as? If you're going to be a zombie dripping rotten meat, I don't want you around."

"That wasn't even me! That was my friend Alex!"

Maya laughed. "I know. What are you going as this year?"

"A fox. Mom helped me put it together."

"Sure. You can come with us."

"Us?" He looked uncertain.

"My plans aren't firm," she said, "but I invited Benjamin and Gwenda. They've never trick-or-treated before. And I asked this girl from school named Helen, but she didn't say yes yet. There's this other girl I might have to ask just because she's lonely." If she invited Sibyl, that would cause all kinds of problems, Maya realized, but . . . "And"—Maya glanced around the living room, then leaned close—"Rimi's coming," she whispered.

"Yaaay!"

"I mean, she couldn't *not* come, but we're going to try to make her my costume."

"Yaaay! But how the heck could that work?"

"We don't know yet. I'm going to have to get some alone time to figure it out."

"Oh, boy!" Peter stood up. "Thanks, Maya," he said, and raced off.

# TWENTY-FOUR

Thanks to Rimi's alarm abilities, Maya actually got to school early Friday morning, before the Janus House kids. She was sitting on a swing in the playground watching cars pull in and drop off kids when Helen sat on the swing next to her. "I'll go trick-or-treating with you, if it's okay if some of my other friends come," Helen said.

"My little brother's coming, and maybe Benjamin and Gwenda," Maya said.

"Benjamin and Gwenda? I've *never* heard of them doing anything on Halloween! This I have to see."

"What's the best neighborhood for candy?"

"Where do you live?" Helen asked.

"Thirty-third, off Passage Street. Next door to Janus House."

"Right near here. Well, your neighborhood is about the best we have, aside from Janus House, which never gives out anything. You'd think it would be a perfect place to get stuff, with so many apartments in one spot, but they turn off the lights and lock the doors. Nobody's ever gotten a thing out of them. People talk about tricking them, but somehow it never happens."

"Would you like to start at my house?" asked Maya. "I don't know where you live."

"Twenty-eight Twelve Slip Street. About five blocks from you. I'm going with Janine and Tovah and Sibyl. You guys meet us at my house at about six, okay? We'll head back to your house. I know the best houses on the way."

"All right. I'm pretty sure that'll be okay. Could I get your phone number in case there's a change in plans?"

They got out cell phones and programmed each other's numbers into them.


"Hey," Travis said as people settled into their homeroom desks, "these two Janus House girls, Alira and Jemmy, came over yesterday afternoon and asked me how to take care of Oma."

"Wow," said Maya. "How'd it go?"

"They were great. Oma liked them. And they were stronger than I am, and they were all, like, we *so* want to help you! to Oma, and they said—"

"What?" Maya asked as Benjamin sat on her other side, with Gwenda settling beyond him.

"They said they'd come over on Halloween so I could go out if I wanted to."

"Wow!"

"So, like, do I want to?"

Maya cocked her head. *Why is he asking me?*

*Tell him he wants to,* Rimi thought.

"You want to," Maya said. She turned toward Benjamin. "You guys are coming, too, right?"

"Yes," said Benjamin. "There's this closet downstairs that's full of clothes. It's for travelers going to different cultures, different worlds, travelers who might need disguises, including some people my size. We have stuff from more than a hundred years ago in there, and I found some great pieces for my costume."

"Your costume?" said Travis.

Benjamin grinned. "Pirate. Maya said."

"Pirate?" Gwenda said. She smiled, too.

"What are you going to be?" Travis asked her.

Gwenda folded her arms and lifted her head. "I'm going to be a witch."

"Whoa!" said Travis.

"Maybe one of those witches with long noses and warts!"

"Whoa!" Travis turned to Maya. "What about you?"

"I haven't worked out my costume yet. I mean, I know what I want it to be, but I'm not sure how to do it yet. But—I should tell you—I asked Helen if we could go with her, and she said yes. And she's got some friends who are going with us, too. Including Sibyl." Maya looked toward Helen and Sibyl, several rows up, who were talking to each other, red-blonde head next to brunette. Sibyl wore a brown dress today. Yiliss gleamed golden around Sibyl's neck.

"Wait a sec," said Benjamin.

"That's not going to be as much fun, going with people we have to keep secrets from," Gwenda said.

"Peter's coming, too."

"Hey!" said Benjamin.

"I'm sorry, you guys," Maya said. "I didn't know you'd

feel this way about it. I wasn't even sure you were coming. And whatever happens, Peter was always coming with us. Otherwise he'd be stuck in grown-up hell, having to have the parents take him around."

"Don't get all bent about it," Travis said. "A bunch of people running around in costumes. All kinds of fun without even getting that weird. Plus, the whole candy thing. What am I going to wear?"

"Come look in the closet after training today," Benjamin said.

Travis's smile spread into a grin. "Okay!"

Mr. Ferrell started taking attendance and everybody quieted down. Sibyl glanced back at Maya, eyebrows up. Maya gave her a finger wave, and Sibyl smiled. Yiliss's fringe flickered.

"You're friends with *her* now?" Travis muttered, looking down at his social studies textbook.

"It's complicated," Maya muttered back. "Tell you later."

At lunch, Benjamin sat with Travis and his eighth-grade friends. Maya watched them covertly from the Janus House table. Travis's friends were all bigger than Benjamin, and it seemed like they were teasing him, but he was smiling and talking back. None of it looked mean. It made Benjamin sparkle in a new way.

She glanced toward Helen's table, where Sibyl sat with Janine and Tovah. Helen, Janine, and Tovah were having some kind of lively discussion. Sibyl sucked a protein drink very slowly, not taking the straw out of her mouth long enough to talk. Yiliss was trying to sneak a fringe down into the can and Sibyl kept flicking him away from it. All the other girls laughed, and Sibyl lowered her drink and smiled at them. She looked so lost.

"Maya. Maya. Earth to Maya," said Twyla, next to her. She snapped her fingers in front of Maya's face.

"Huh?"

"I said, what is going on here? Why is Ben at some other table today? What's all this about Halloween?"

Rowan said, "None of that is important. Tell us more about Sibyl and her *sissimi*."

"Not here," Maya said. "Not now."

"What's that? I never heard that part!" Twyla glanced at Sibyl.

"Don't look," Maya whispered.

Twyla turned and picked up her bread cup, scraping at

it with her spoon, her attention all in front of her. "What is that about?" she muttered.

Gwenda gripped Maya's wrist. "Yes, Maya, what is that about?" she asked in a low voice.

*Shock her?* Rimi wondered.

*No. But thanks.*

"I didn't know who Columba would tell," Maya murmured. She left her wrist in Gwenda's grip and used her other hand to feel in her brown paper lunch bag, hoping for something else to eat, but she'd already scarfed her PBJ and Twinkies and the apple she'd packed last night. She wadded up the bag. "I feel like I shouldn't be talking about this here. Honestly."

Gwenda turned to Kallie, silent so far. "Kallie, did you know?"

"Yes," she said. "Columba told us. Probably she was telling Rowan most, but she let me hear, too."

"Sibyl has a *sissimi*," Gwenda muttered.

"I found out yesterday. I feel like a bad person, telling people when it's her secret, but I thought Columba should know. I thought the people looking for the lost *sissimi* should know."

"Sibyl has a *sissimi* and she's coming trick-or-treating with us?" Gwenda asked.

Maya shrugged. "It sort of fell together that way."

"This holiday is just getting weirder and weirder," said Twyla.

"I'm coming with you," Rowan said.

"What? No. Nobody wants you," Maya said. She put her hand over her mouth, but it was too late to keep the words inside.

The eye Maya could see past his hair narrowed. Red touched his cheek. "That doesn't matter," he said after too long a pause. "I'm coming."

Sarutha met Maya at the bottom of the Janus House Apartments' staircase after school. Maya glanced toward Columba's door, then crossed the entry hall to join Sarutha. They went up to Sarutha's jewel apartment and Sarutha poured tea for both of them. Carrying their teacups, they went out to the balcony. It was cold and overcast. The last leaves were falling. Maya smelled damp on the air, and the spice of crushed, dried leaves. She felt an autumn melancholy. She had the feeling this might be the last time she and Sarutha had beverages on the balcony together.

"Namdi, are you handing me over to Columba now?" she asked when she and Sarutha had seated themselves with steaming teacups warming their hands.

"Won't that suit you better?" Sarutha asked.

"What if I said no?"

"We would try to respect that, Maya, my dear, but everybody in the family finds their work and does it, and the sooner the better. We will try to be patient with you as you find your place. It's just that the indicators are so clear: security is where you belong. We know it's not the way of the outside world, at least in this country, to have children find their callings so young, but we have always done it this way."

"You're not my First Family," Maya said. She had a flash of desire to run back to her parents and her brother and sister and have them all move away, anywhere but here. She was twelve. She didn't want a career. She wanted to have summer to play, and fall, winter, and spring to learn. She wanted to be a kid.

"We try to respect that," Sarutha said.

*They can't make us do anything we don't want to do,* Rimi thought fiercely. *I'll stop them.*

*I don't know if we can fight everything they can do, especially if they have people like Ara-Kita and Kachik-Vati on their side.*

*Ara-Kita and Kachik-Vati are on our side, not theirs.*

*Are you sure?*

*I'm sure of Kita and Vati,* Rimi thought. *Do you want to fight this now?*

*I*—Maya sighed and sipped tea—*No. I like Columba, anyway.*

*So do I. And we have each other. They don't really understand that yet.*

*Might be better to keep that to ourselves.*

Rimi sent a smile.

Maya set down her teacup and hugged herself, including Rimi in the embrace. Rimi wrapped her in answering warmth. *Whatever happens, we will have choices,* Rimi thought.

*Thank you, Rimi. Thank you.*

"Maya, my dear," Sarutha said. She stroked Maya's hair.

Maya looked at her watch. "Time for principles of magic," she said. She stood up and shrugged into her backpack.

Sarutha rose, too, set down her cup. "Maya," she said softly, and opened her arms.

Maya closed her eyes and let Sarutha's hug enfold her. For the past six weeks she had been working with Sarutha three afternoons a week before she went to her other classes, discussing everything magical, following Sarutha through the huge pile of Janus House and the warren of secret places beneath it. Sarutha had been patient and pleasant, answering Maya's many questions. She had been a good guide and guardian. She had felt trustworthy and safe to Maya.

Sarutha smelled like black tea and roses, talcum powder and sunlight. Her arms were thin and strong and warm. "I'm not going anywhere," she murmured against Maya's hair. "You'll just be too busy to see me."

"Maybe," Maya said, and eased out of Sarutha's embrace. She went to the door of the apartment, stood on the threshold and looked back, memorizing the open cages, the reaching plants, the cloudy sky beyond the balcony doors, the spidery velvet silhouette of the old woman against the light. She lifted her hand, stepped out, and shut the door behind her.

# TWENTY-FIVE

Principles of Magic class let out early. Maya had
not been able to make "Catch and Hold" work any better
than the previous five techniques the teacher had taught
them. She had felt completely helpless as each of the Littles
caught her and made her stand still. It had involved a phrase
in Kerlinqua and some complicated hand gestures, both of
which Maya could perform perfectly, the teacher said. Even
the Littles who couldn't get the pronunciation quite right
made the technique work for them. They spent a lot of time
giggling and practicing on each other.

*I could have caught and held them,* Rimi said. *And they
didn't catch* me, *not even once.*

*Maybe next time,* Maya thought. Then she thought,

*Maybe we don't need a next time. I'm tired of seeing all the things these kids can do that I'll never be able to master.*

*I want to know,* Rimi thought. *Once I know what's possible, I will figure out how to do it. We will have all these powers, Maya.*

Maya sighed. She paused outside Columba's apartment, then lifted her hand and knocked on the door.

Columba opened the door. She looked frazzled. "Maya," she said. "Just the person I need! Come in."

In the kitchen, a pot of tea steamed on the table, and Evren sat in one of the chairs, futzing with thin strips of metal, wires, pliers, and a little silver hammer. He looked up and smiled. "Hey, Maya. Hey, Rimi," he said. "Oh, good."

"What?"

"We're trying to develop a *sissimi* detector," Columba said. Evren held up a mess of woven metal strips and wires. He took one of the loose metal strips and attached it at the top, with a wire piercing its center so it looked like a badly designed propeller.

He sang a short phrase to it three times, and it whirled around, then stopped, quivering, with one end pointing toward Maya. "Ha!" he said.

"Fantastic," said Columba.

Rimi reached for it. *It is*— she began. Maya sensed her filtering into the device, weaving between its parts. *Oh! Oh! This tastes—it is all* filisizz! Rimi fluttered with delight.

The propeller whirled so madly it fell off.

"What?" Evren said. He shook the device.

Rimi laughed and escaped from it.

"She went into it," Maya said.

"Oh. Yeah, it wasn't set up for that. Guess I better build in that parameter." He retrieved the propeller from the floor and fitted it back onto the shaft. It spun toward Maya again. "All right, now I just have to clean it up."

"What kind of range do you think it'll have?" Columba asked.

"No way to tell until we field test it."

"Maya," Columba said.

"I guess we could go outside and I could walk away and see how far I go before the detector stops pointing toward you," Evren said. "That would be good data."

"Once you establish that," Columba said, "I'd really like Maya use the detector to sense that Sibyl girl's *sissimi*. If we could track her that way—"

"Maya can't do that," Evren said. "She has Rimi."

"Oh, right. Maybe we can get Rowan or Benjamin to try

it in school. Maya, you were the answer to my mind's prayer, but maybe you had some other reason for stopping by?"

Maya slumped into the kitchen chair opposite Evren's. "Sarutha said . . ."

Columba sat next to her and laid a hand on her shoulder. "What is it?" she asked gently.

Maya put her hands over her face. "I can't learn principles of magic, and I can't sing things into doing what I want. I can pronounce things and gesture and sing right, but they don't work."

"Not all of us can use those disciplines," Columba said. She rubbed her hand up and down Maya's upper arm and shoulder.

"I'm not like *any* of you. I don't have magic inside me."

"You do," said Columba. "You have the magic of observation and recall. You see things, and you can summon their images afterward."

Maya lowered her hands and stared at Columba.

"That's a wonderful magic," Columba said, "and Rimi has other skills, no? Look what she did to the detector. She can pick things up at a distance, too, and bring them to you. I wonder what the weight limit is on her lifting ability . . . we could test. . . . You two have the makings of a terrific criminal."

"I don't want to be a criminal," Maya said, and thought, *You don't know the half of it.*

"Well," said Columba, "it's not a crime if you do it as part of our security force."

Maya crossed her arms and stared at the floor. Then she closed her eyes. *Rimi, what about this? What about having Columba for our teacher instead of Sarutha? What about our doing this kind of sneaking?*

*I love anything that will give me more information,* Rimi thought. *Sarutha has been good to you, but lately all she does is tell you what you can't do. And she doesn't know what we* can *do. She's not even asking the right questions. At least Columba notices* me.

*Okay, I like that part of it, too, although it might make it harder for us to keep our own secrets.* "I don't want to do things that are wrong," Maya said aloud.

"I can work with that," Columba said. "As long as you understand that protecting our family and the portals is right."

"I—I want to be able to say no if you ask me to do things that feel wrong." Maya hated how Harper had been able to force her to do things. She didn't want another Harper in her life.

Columba reached for Maya's hand. Columba's hand was

large and rough and warm. Her grip was comforting and strong. "*Akala*, you will always be able to say no. Sometimes we won't respect your no, but I will do my best to try. We will open that portal when we come to it. Join my force. We have cake."

"Really?" Maya asked.

Evren lifted a cake plate out of the refrigerator. It held half a round of brown two-layer spice cake, covered on top with creamy frosting, and smelling of cinnamon, ginger, nutmeg, cloves, and palta. "Dr. Porta baked this morning. Want some?"

Maya gripped Columba's hand and released it. "Yes," she said, to everything.

After cake, the promise of a meeting after school on Monday, a request from Columba that Maya walk past Dreams & Bones sometime over the weekend and sketch what she saw through the window as her first security assignment, and a strange settling inside as Maya adjusted her expectations, Maya thought, *Now let's go to the woods and work on our Halloween costume.*

*Yesss!* Rimi low-fived, slapping an invisible hand against Maya's.

Maya watched for Travis as she left Janus House, but he was still in class, apparently. She headed to the park.

People were walking their dogs along the bike path. Rimi practiced spreading calm to dogs who sensed her and started barking. She was a pro now at getting them to accept her.

They reached the woods, checked for possible watchers, and plunged in. The hideout in the middle of the blackberry vines was undisturbed since their last visit. Maya settled on the damp ground.

*Halloween*, Rimi thought. *I've never been there, but I like everything about it already. How are you going to dress as me?*

*I thought—if you can make an arm, could you make a head?*

*A head!* Rimi pressed invisible hands all over Maya's head, pushing Maya's hair flat to her skull, gliding her hands over Maya's cheeks, nose, forehead, cupping the ears, patting the mouth. *Different from an arm. Not as useful!*

*Sure, sure, mock my brains*, Maya thought. *Anyway, you wouldn't have to put a brain in it, just make it* look *like a head. Though I was thinking it would be really cool if it could function. Like, what if you could talk out loud? You could talk to Peter!*

*Tempting*, Rimi thought. *Where would I put it?*

Maya patted her shoulder.

*No, the right confluence isn't there. It wouldn't connect right. I don't think I could make it talk. At least, not like a human talks.*

"The thing about Halloween is it doesn't matter if it works, just how it looks," Maya said.

*You would be wobbly and off-balance if I put a head on one shoulder. Maybe if I put two heads, one on each shoulder—*

Maya got out her sketchbook and two pencils.

Saturday morning Maya went down to the kitchen to look for her mother, who was drinking coffee and reading a novel, wearing her relaxed weekend clothes: jeans and a baggy green T-shirt with WILLAMETTE VALLEY FOLK FESTIVAL on it above a sketch of a fiddler.

"What is it, honey?" Mom asked.

"I know it's really, really late, Mom, but I finally figured out my costume, and I wondered if you could help me make it."

"Sure! What did you come up with?"

"I want to be a warrior. Like, an ancient Greek, with a shield and some armor." She put her sketchbook on the table and flipped to the most recent pictures she and Rimi had worked on. They had stopped at the library before they ran into Friday afternoon curfew, and studied some pictures in books. "I thought I could make a kind of tunic thing out of sheets and then use pieces of cardboard for the armor on top of it. I need to get some silver spray paint."

"A warrior, Maya?" Mom sounded uneasy.

"Not because I want to fight, Mom, just because it's neat. I can wear my black waffle-weave shirt and jeans under the tunic chiton thing, and—"

Mom frowned. "There's no magic in it."

Maya didn't understand at first. She looked at her sketch. This was a working sketch, showing all the boring parts of the costume. Simple sheets, pinned together along the tops of the arms, belted at the waist; cut-out cardboard shapes tied on with twine—

Oh. Every previous year, Maya and Stephanie had chosen magical costumes.

"I'm going to draw Medusa's head on the shield," Maya said. Stephanie had been crazy about Greek myths. "And my friend is letting me borrow the coolest helmet ever."

Mom studied the sketch. "This is seriously what you want, honey?"

"Yep."

"Okay, then. We've got all those moving boxes in the garage we can cut up, and I have a pair of sheets on their last legs. You want some nice white flannel sheets with red hearts on them?"

"No," Maya said.

Mom laughed. "I figured. We have those dark blue ones with light blue stars. How about those?"

In the pictures they'd studied, the Roman guys wore red tunics under their armor, and the Greek guys wore white tunics, but those were just speculations, Maya guessed, and anyway, she wasn't going for accuracy. "Sounds great."

"I'll warm up the sewing machine. There's a couple of box cutters in the tool drawer. Let's do this thing."

Later that afternoon, Maya stood against the wall outside Dreams & Bones, then leaned over to peek through the wide front window. People, a mix of kids and grown-ups, sat at tables in the café, some talking with each other, others reading or laptopping or netbooking. The pastries lined up in front of the window looked delicious, shiny glazed sugar swirls over the baked brown and gleaming jewel jelly of the Danishes, the bear claws wide and resplendent with slivered almonds and whip lines of white frosting, all kinds of doughnuts, cookies, scones, brownies, even some thick slices of heavily frosted cake.

Maya straightened, leaning against the building's brick wall, and lifted her sketchpad. *Could you hold this for me?* she thought.

*Sure.* Rimi rippled down Maya's arms and slid under the sketchbook, supporting it while Maya penciled a quick drawing of the interior. *Thanks,* Maya thought. She glanced both ways along the sidewalk, ready to grab the sketchbook if anybody looked her way. Cars passed in the street, but no one was paying attention to her.

Maya leaned in for another peek. She had the foreground; now she needed the depths of the store.

The owner was staring at her from behind the pastry display.

"Ulp." She ducked back. She grabbed the sketchpad from Rimi and hugged it to her chest.

*Something,* Rimi thought. *Something, Mayamela. Something I remember. Let's go inside.*

*He saw me!*

*Yes,* Rimi thought. *A girl looking in a window. He has probably seen such a thing before.*

Maya hugged her sketchbook and took three deep breaths, huffing them in and out through her nose. She sighed and stepped away from the wall, stowed her sketch-pad in her backpack, and headed for the store's entrance.

*He can't hurt you, Maya. I am with you.*

*Yes,* Maya thought. She pulled on the handle, a wrought-iron dragon whose twisted tail formed the grip. Bells jangled as she opened the door. Well, she'd get a better view of the place from inside, and maybe she could snag one of the tables and do her sketching without enlisting Rimi's help.

"What can I help you find?" said a warm, deep voice from her left. It sounded furry, and had a faint accent, though Maya wasn't sure if it was French or Spanish or Other.

She glanced up. It was the proprietor, and he was smiling faintly. "I don't—" she began.

*I know this person!* Rimi thought. *It is the one who troubled my other Other. Maya! He is the one who talked to Bikos and told him to look otherwise than to the Thrixa for help when we were so sick.*

*This one?* Maya looked carefully at the proprietor's face, stared into his eyes even as she felt her attention trying to shift. There was a flutter in his irises, which had looked black to her before. Now she saw silvery sparks there, surrounding pupils that were diamond-shaped.

"Ah," he said. He cocked his head, the movement strange, as though his neck had a few extra vertebrae.

"I think you knew my friend Bikos," Maya said in a low voice.

"Yes," he said, "and his friend who is with you now."

Maya backed up, her hand reaching for the door handle.

*Please*, Rimi thought. *Please don't run away, Maya.*

*But he knows about you! And he's—he's not human.*

*Lots of people aren't.*

"Tea," said the man.

"What?"

"I have a spice tea called Dragon's Fire. I think you'll like it. There's a room in the back where I practice the fortune-telling arts. We could talk in private."

Maya tightened her grip on the dragon door handle, a match to the one on the outside of the door. The iron was cool and hard against her fingers and palm. Rimi flowed a little across her back, waiting.

"All right," Maya said.

The man turned his gaze from her. "Stuart," he called, "could you watch the register?"

"Sure," said a tall, stocky guy with black-framed glasses and a pirate's smile. He set down the manga he had been reading and moved behind the bookstore counter.

The proprietor went behind the coffeeshop counter, poured steaming water into a teapot, assembled a tray, and carried it toward the back of the store. Maya followed him. Mindful of her security job, she looked everywhere, noting the shelves, the patrons, the goods. Kids lounged, sprawled, sat on the floor, absorbed in comics and books. At a table near the back wall, kids rolled many-sided dice and played cards with anime characters on them. People looked comfortable here.

The door the man led her through was thick wood painted burgundy red. It had steel rivets on it in a Greek key pattern. As Maya stepped over the threshold into the room beyond, she felt an electric tingling. She stepped back into the store. It stopped.

"Oh," said the man. "Sorry." He tapped the door's edge and muttered, then nodded.

Maya stepped over the threshold again, and this time nothing happened.

The room had a round table in its center, covered with a dark purple velvet cloth. A crystal ball rested on a wooden stand in the middle of the table. One red, upholstered chair sat on the far side of the table, and another stood with its back to Maya. The light was dim. The walls were papered with dark patterns. There were no windows. The scent of incense lingered.

"Close the door," said the man. He set the tea tray next to the crystal ball and sat in the chair on the far side of the table.

Maya turned the doorknob. It moved freely. Not locked. She pulled the door shut—all the store noise of conversation vanished—and sat in the second chair.

"I'm Weyland," said the man. He poured two cups of tea and held one out to her. They weren't regular teacups, more like small earthenware mugs.

"Thank you." Maya accepted the cup and sniffed the tea. Mint and lime and hickory smoke. She set the cup on the velvet and looked at Weyland.

"And you are not Bikos," he said.

Should she tell him her name? She hesitated, then said, "No. Sorry. I'm Maya."

"Peter's sister."

"Yeah."

"Travis's best friend."

"His *best* friend?"

"He hasn't said that, but I infer it. He mentioned you often before he became too busy to stop in after school. Did Bikos—"

Maya shook her head and looked away.

"I wish I could have helped him more. The medicine I know did not work on him." Weyland drank tea and poured himself a second cup. "He found a way for his friend to survive without him, yes?"

*Rimi, how can I talk to him about you? I don't know him.*

*He is why we found each other.*

*Does that automatically make him a good guy?*

Rimi dropped a tentacle into the teacup and sampled Dragon's Fire tea. The smoky taste flowed across Maya's tongue. She swallowed, then said, "What did you say to him?"

He smiled sadly at her. Maybe that was why she hadn't been able to look into his eyes before: not because they were alien, but because he was so sad, and Maya had been feeling enough of her own sad she hadn't wanted anybody else's. He said, "I had a friend once whom I wanted to save, and I gave her to the wrong people, thinking they would help her, but they hurt her instead."

"Why did Bikos even ever talk to you about any of this?"

"I gave him shelter here for a few days, and I fed him, though the food didn't do him much good. I take in strays when they let me. He had a terrible dilemma. Maya, we don't know each other at all, but I see—" He paused. He stroked a hand over the crystal ball. Something glimmered in its center. "You have saved his friend. The people who left him here would have hurt her, even if Bikos had lived. Even now, they are trying to find her. She is wearing a little red feather that glows like a beacon telling them where she is."

"She is?" *Oh, no! Is this the red thorn?*

*Ask him how we can remove it.*

"How can we get rid of it?" Maya asked.

"I don't think my medicine will work on that, either, but—" He opened a drawer in the table and rummaged, then held up a little silver pendant shaped like a lifted hand, fingers up and palm facing out. "Here." He held it out to her.

*Rimi.* Maya opened her hand.

Rimi reached ahead of her, lifting the pendant. It floated above Weyland's hand. *I* fenshu *it. It tastes—*

Maya tasted warm, buttered bread. And then a sliver of ice.

*I love this! Inside is one thing, and outside, another!* Rimi thought.

"If you wear it, it will dim the red feather." He rummaged in the drawer again and came up with a silver chain. He held it up, and Rimi took it from him and threaded it through the pendant's loop. Weyland didn't seem to find anything strange about a pendant floating in the air, or a chain snaking through the air to join it.

Rimi brought the pendant to Maya, who caught it in her hand and studied it. The silver hand was detailed and beautiful, and it had six fingers. *Is it safe?* she wondered.

*Yes*, Rimi thought. *Yes, please, yes. I will put it on you.*

Maya blew out a breath and lifted her hair away from her neck. Rimi fastened the chain. The pendant slid inside Maya's shirt collar to lie at the top of her sternum.

Weyland nodded once. "Yes. The glow subsides."

"Thank you," Maya said. "Do I—do you want—I didn't get my allowance yet this week—"

"No payment, Maya, except perhaps you help someone else." He rose. "You are a girl of many secrets. Will you keep mine?"

"I—" Columba had sent her here to learn about Weyland and the store. What was she going to tell her new mentor?

Her first chance to say no, she guessed. "I'll do my best."

He held out his hand, and she clasped it. His grip was warm, strong, and gentle. Rimi wrapped around his hand, too, and he smiled.

"Can I show them sketches of the store?" she asked when he released her.

"Oh, yes."

"They can't see in, you know," she said, and then she wondered if he knew she was talking about the Janus House people.

He seemed to. He smiled even wider. "I wanted to delay their knowledge of me as long as I could, but they're alert now, and I'll have to find another way to hide what's truly important from them. Maya. If you need to talk to some-one outside the system—" He moved past her and opened the door, and the room filled with the noise of other people again. "I'll be here."

"Thank you," she said again. She pressed her hand over the new pendant, which was warm against her skin. "Thank you."

Music Night the night before Halloween started out differ-ently. Maya was unfolding chairs and setting them around the living room when Great-uncle Harper came up the porch steps, flanked by Sarutha and Noona. Mom and Dad met them at the door, then looked beyond for the usual crowd. Maya paused, too, and looked. No one followed the Elders.

"Mrs. Andersen, Mr. Andersen, we need to talk," Great-uncle Harper said. "It's getting too cold to sit outside."

"I'd been thinking that myself," said Dad. "We've been trying to heat the whole outdoors, but it hasn't worked. We don't want people getting sick just to sing."

"Nor do we," said Great-uncle Harper. "We were thinking we might come in more manageable numbers until it gets warm again. We'll take turns joining you."

"I'm sure we'll miss those who can't make it," Mom said, "but it might work better that way. Unless you folks have a big room somewhere in Janus House we could all fit in."

"We have some large rooms, but none large enough for that," said Harper.

Maya thought of two rooms big enough without even trying: the portal room and the central courtyard where the Janus House people had held an interportal council with lots of aliens right after Maya had first acquired Rimi. Couldn't let the family see either of those places, she guessed.

"Are you the only ones coming tonight?" Mom asked Harper.

Sarutha said, "No. We are the delegation to check with you to see whether you are all right with the change of plans."

"Sure," said Mom.

"I will go back and fetch tonight's contingent," said Noona, peeling off.

Mom and Dad stood back. "Please come in," Dad said to Harper and Sarutha.

"There was one other thing," Harper said

"How can we help you?" Dad asked.

"Halloween," said Harper.

"What about it?"

"Maya invited some of our youngsters to go out and terrorize the neighbors. We don't do that."

"What?" Mom said.

"He's talking about trick-or-treating, Mom," Maya said.

Just then, Peter came down the stairs wearing his fox head, which was one of the best masks Mom had ever made: a broad red face, with a long red snout with black whiskers and a black nose on the end, upstanding black ears with tufts of pale fur inside, a white chin, and shiny yellow eyes.

Harper startled, though Sarutha smiled. "What is that?" Harper demanded.

"That's Peter," said Mom.

"It's part of my costume, Mr. Harper," Peter said, his voice muffled behind the mask.

"Why are the children dressing up as something they're not?" Harper asked.

"It's just play, Mr. Harper," Mom said. "I don't think there's any harm in it."

Harper looked stern. Maya's grip tightened on the back of the folding chair she had just put in place. What if he cast some kind of spell?

Sarutha poked him in the side. "Play, Harper. Play."

"I don't like it," Harper said.

Dad said, "Well, we wouldn't presume to tell other parents how to raise their children. If it troubles you that much, I'm sure your children can stay home."

Sarutha poked Harper again. He brushed her hand aside and said, "No, no. I'm sure the children will survive it. I just worry. Excuse me." He turned and went out to stand on the edge of the porch. He waved a hand toward Janus House, and then the usual flood of chattering happy people carrying instruments and refreshments materialized, except there were half the usual number.

# MEETING

They all fit inside the Andersen house, without even bumping elbows the way they usually did. With the doors and windows shut, they sounded even better and more concentrated than they had before.

Benjamin, Gwenda, and Rowan didn't come.

# TWENTY-SIX

Maya went outside to collect her armor Sunday afternoon. She and her mother had set the cut-out cardboard pieces, stiffened and curved appropriately with the aid of papier-mâché, on newspapers on the porch Saturday afternoon and sprayed them with a lot of silver paint. They had dried well, without too many drips, and they looked pretty darned good, Maya thought. Breastplate, backplate, shield, and greaves/shin guards.

She grabbed the shield—which she had made out of six cardboard rounds Superglued to each other to stiffen it, with luggage straps stapled on the back for her arm to slide through—and the breastplate. At the kitchen table, she got out a fat black Sharpie and drew a Medusa head on the shield, with lots of snakes for hair. Somehow, Medusa's face ended up looking like Stephanie's, not glaring like a monster, but smiling, as though she liked having such active hair.

On the breastplate, Maya drew some fancy curlicues like the ones she'd seen in pictures of Greek soldiers.

Her mother came in. "Nice," she said. She held up the tunic she had made from one of the sheets. Instead of falling full length, it was a short tunic, going to mid-thigh. "Black jeans under it? It's supposed to be cold tonight."

"Yeah. I can tie the greaves on over my jeans. I've got to go borrow the helmet." Rimi said Maya had the correct confluences for attachment on the back of her neck. Maya and Rimi had tried various helmets based on the pictures they'd studied, which showed some crazy headgear. Rimi liked one that showed the helmet as a monster's head with a wide mouth open around Maya's face, as though the monster had just bitten down on Maya's head and hadn't started chewing yet. Ultimately, they chose an Athena helmet, because Athena often wore her helmet pushed up on her head. Maya ended up having another face above her own.

Candra came in, heading for the refrigerator. She stopped and studied Maya's armor. "Cool, little sister."

Mom said, "What kind of loot bag are you going to carry? Anything normal will make the outfit look ridiculous."

"Loot bag. I *knew* I forgot something!"

"I know," said Candra. "I've got that old black messenger bag. You could take that. Are you going to have a sword?"

"A sword," Maya said. "D'oh!"

"Probably better if you don't. It'll just get in the way."

"Most of the guys on vases had javelins, anyway."

"Who do you imagine you're fighting?" Candra asked.

"Nobody, really." *Everybody who wants to lock us into doing or being something we don't want.* "We just want to look excellent."

"What is this 'we'?" asked Candra.

Maya hesitated. "Me and my shadow."

"Cryptic!" Candra said.

Maya put on her costume around five thirty. The cardboard parts were a little tricky, but the helmet took the longest, even though they had practiced after lights-out the night before.

*I'm staring at the ceiling*, Rimi thought.

"Maybe you can tilt forward a little. Reshape the face."

Maya studied the helmet in the mirror. It had a domed top, with a little owl perching on it. Blank eye holes stared upward, and there was a nasal piece, and a mouth—none of the pictures they looked at had mouths, but the whole point was so Rimi could talk if she wanted to, so they had changed the design.

Maya tried shifting the helmet forward. It was not hollow inside, but filled with Rimi stuff. More dense than a scarf, but light, and infinitely adjustable. Rimi shifted her mass to the new angle.

"You don't actually need to look out the eyeholes, do you?" Maya asked. Rimi saw everything, and she didn't usually have eyes.

*Just wanted to try it. I'm pretending I have a head tonight. This is a little better. Plus, I can use the owl's eyes.* The owl's eyes glowed golden. One of them winked.

"Do we make sense together?" Maya spread her arms and looked at her costume. She was in black and silver, with the dark blue starry tunic in between. The silver helmet made her head look strange and large, but it wasn't a bad look.

*I think we do.*

Maya went to her dresser and looked at the pictures

of Stephanie. She ran her finger through the little bowl of raw garnets she and Stephanie had collected in a creek in northern Idaho, back when they went hiking with their families on a regular basis. She picked out the biggest one and slipped it into her jeans change pocket.

Someone knocked on the door. Before she could say "wait," a fox walked in. It had a cream chest and belly, but the rest of it was red fur, except for black hands and feet and the tip of its tail. Its tail was bushy and beautiful.

"I hate when you do that," Maya said.

"I know," said Peter, muffled through the fox's head, "but I keep forgetting."

"Well, you're annoying, but you look great."

"You, too. You about ready?"

Maya looked at Rimi in the mirror again. "Are we ready?"

"Ready," said the helmet. Rimi's voice sounded like a younger version of Maya's.

Peter jumped.

"Hi, Peter!" Rimi said.

"Ri-Ri-*Rimi*?" His voice changed with each syllable.

"I'm going to look out of the owl eyes. I can point them different directions." The owl's head swiveled. Its golden eyes gleamed.

Peter took off his fox head and stared.

"Isn't she awesome?" Maya asked.

"Oh, yeah," said Peter. "Wow." He came closer, staring at Maya's helmet. "Wow, Rimi. Wow! Can I try you on?"

"Um, no, Peter. I'm attached to Maya's neck."

"Ewww!"

"But at least I can talk to you."

"My first conversation with an alien," Peter said. "Now I feel like I have to say something smart."

"Me, too," said Rimi. "Let's not. Anyway, we won't be able to talk long, because all these people who don't know about me are going to be walking around with us. But I wanted to at least say hi to you now. Hi!"

"Hi! Can I touch you?"

Maya bent over, her hands going to the helmet to make sure it stayed on. *You don't have to worry,* Rimi thought. *I won't fall off. I don't want to, and anyway, I'm attached, remember?* Rimi flexed something that made a circular section of the back of Maya's neck pulse and sparkle.

Peter put his hand on the helmet's cheekpiece. "Soft," he said. "Looks like silver. Feels like velvet. This is confusing."

"I don't think anybody else is going to touch me. I can be harder if I have to," Rimi said. She did something and was suddenly heavier. Maya patted her and felt the hard coolness of metal. Peter touched it, too, his eyes widening.

"But I think that might give Maya a headache!" Rimi changed back. "Put your head on, Fox Boy, and let's go."

"Rimi," Peter said. He blinked up at the little owl, then put on his mask.

At the front door, Mom, Dad, and Candra waited.

"Maya! It's magnificent!" Mom said.

Candra swung her camera up. "You guys are the best dressed trick-or-treaters ever! This is a great year for Andersen costumes. You guys rule!" She snapped picture after picture. "Pose a little more, will you? Maya, that helmet, oh my God. Where'd it come from?"

"My best friend loaned it to me."

"Who's your best friend?" Candra asked.

Maya paused. Land mines underfoot when you least expected them. "Rimi," she said.

"Not Gwenda?" asked Mom.

"I think I have a bunch of best friends now," Maya said.

"When can we meet Rimi?"

"Um," said Maya. *Rimi?*

*I can work on a body if you want me to. I have a shadow self. I could just color it in. But it has to stay attached to you. I don't know if this is a good idea.*

"Maybe later?" Maya said.

"Does she live next door?"

"No. She's someone I met in school."

"Later." Mom nodded. "For now, just have fun. I have to say, I like her taste in clothes."

"Do you have your cell phones?" asked Dad.

Maya dug her phone out of her pocket and held it up.

Peter shrugged. "Can I use Maya's?"

"If you both swear on your direst oaths you won't get separated," Mom said.

"I do so swear," Maya and Peter said.

"Flashlights," said Dad. He handed each of them a pocket-size LED flashlight. Maya put hers in the opposite pocket from the cell phone and her house keys. Peter tucked his into a pocket, too. How cool was that? Mom had made the fox outfit with pockets.

"You need loot bags," said Candra. She handed Maya the black messenger bag. Maya had a little trouble getting it on over the helmet; Candra helped her lift it over and tuck it on her right side, where it didn't interfere with the shield on her left arm.

Mom gave Peter a red cloth shopping bag with handles. "Thanks," he said.

"You're going to get cold," Dad said. "I know it'll mess with your costumes, but maybe you should wear jackets."

"I could still be a fox in a jacket," Peter said. He went to the coat closet and got out his puffy winter jacket, dark blue with black stripes down the arms. He slid it on over his fox arms, then held out his hands and turned this way and that. "How does it look?"

Candra took three pictures and showed him one on the digital camera screen. "Pretty good," she said.

"My head will never fit inside the hood," he said.

"But the mask will keep you warm," said Mom.

"I don't think a jacket would work for me," Maya said.

*I'll keep you warm*, Rimi thought.

*I figured.*

"I have my warm stuff on under the tunic," she added. She lifted her wrist and glanced at her watch. "We gotta go!"

"Check in every hour," Dad said. "If you lose track, I'll call you. Call if you need help or a ride or anything. All right?"

"Okay, Dad. Thanks! See you later." Maya grabbed Peter's hand and pulled him out the front door.

A witch, a short pirate, and a tall Christmas tree waited on the sidewalk in front of the house. A little farther away stood a grumpy Rowan, all in black, kind of his everyday clothes, except he was wearing a black hooded cape and carrying a scythe taller than his head. It looked like it was made out of foam rubber.

"Hi!" Maya said. "Rowan, you're Death? Perfect. Have you met my brother, Peter?"

"Hi," said Rowan.

"Hi. I've seen you, but I haven't met you," Peter said.

"You're kind of hard to recognize at the moment," Rowan said.

"That's what Halloween is all about," said Maya.

"*You* look just the same," Rowan said.

"Gee, thanks. Hi, guys!"

Gwenda was in many layers of black: knee-high black boots with pointy toes, a black ruffled skirt, a spiderweb lace jacket over all, and a tall, pointy hat, bent at the top, with a generous brim that had one large spider hanging down. She carried a big tapestry bag, but it was black, not multicolored like her regular one.

Benjamin wore what looked like a knee-length dark leather jacket with large turned-back cuffs and silver coin buttons. Under it he wore a white shirt and a red sash, and he had a tri-corner hat, and knee-high black boots over his jeans. He had drawn on a mustache, but he was still recognizably himself.

"Not disguised?" Maya asked.

He shrugged. "What the heck."

"You look great," Maya told Gwenda and Benjamin. "Travis, why a Christmas tree?"

"Dude. It's not really a Christmas tree," said the Christmas tree. "It's a green *murumrum*."

Maya went closer and studied Travis's costume. It was green and round, pointed at the top and broad at the base, and it really looked like a Christmas tree. The decorations were dangling arms that looked like they'd been taken from Muppets, though, and there were three eyes at the top. Travis's own arms stuck out from the sides and made dents in the circular shape. "Oh," she said. It wasn't really like Kachik-Vati, but it wasn't like much else.

"But I'm just going to say it's a Christmas tree decorated by monsters, in keeping with the Halloween theme. Kinda."

"Okay."

"Maya, you look amazing. But you need a cape!" Gwenda said. She turned and ran back toward Janus House.

"Wait!" Maya called, but Gwenda was already inside.

In two minutes she was back, with a red cloak she fastened around Maya's shoulders.

"Much better," she said.

"Thanks! Now, let's go. We're late!"

The sun was setting, and goblins and ghosts were out on the sidewalk in flocks, shepherded by normally dressed adults. Pumpkins with candles in their mouths burned on porches, along with lighted Halloween decorations— ghosts, skeletons, strings of skull lights, pumpkin lights, bat lights. The air smelled of woodsmoke and cold iron.

Maya dragged her friends past clumps of other kids already scoring big loot. They ran in the street. Fortunately, there was not a lot of traffic at night, but too many other people clogged the sidewalk. Gwenda ran holding onto her hat, her skirts flaring. Rowan held his scythe as though he was ready to slice someone with it. Travis grabbed Maya's arm. "I can't see so good in this thing," he muttered. She gripped his hand and led him. Peter held his tail over his arm. Benjamin ran the easiest; his clothes behaved themselves, and he wasn't carrying anything.

*Evren's following us,* Rimi said, when Maya stopped everyone to let a car drive over a crosswalk.

*Great.*

They were all out of breath by the time they got to Helen's address.

"We're ten minutes late," Maya muttered. "I hope they're still here."

"Kinda hope they're not," muttered Travis.

Maya glanced at him—no way to tell what he was thinking, his face was invisible—and rang the doorbell.

A smiling red-haired Wonder Woman opened the door, letting out warmth and perfume and dinner smells. "You forgot to say trick-or-treat!" She laughed and offered them candy in a wicker basket.

"Are you Mrs. Halloran?" Maya asked. "We were supposed to meet Helen and the others here."

"Oh! Are you Maya? Nice to meet you! Yes, they're in the living room having mulled cider. Would you like some candy anyway?"

"Sure," said Maya. "Thanks."

The basket Mrs. Halloran offered was full of fun-size Milky Ways. Benjamin glanced at Maya. "Take one and say thanks," Maya told him. "It's their first time," she explained to Mrs. Halloran.

"What? That's amazing! All of them?" Mrs. Halloran proffered the basket to each of them in turn.

"No, just the witch, the pirate, and Death. The rest of us have been doing this awhile."

Rowan took a candy bar and turned it back and forth, frowning at it. "Thanks. What do I do with it?"

Benjamin tucked his into one of the big pockets in his jacket. Gwenda held open her tapestry bag. "In here, Rowan."

Mrs. Halloran said, "Who's this delightful little fox?"

"That's my little brother, Peter."

"You are the cutest thing I've seen so far," said Mrs. Halloran. "We haven't had that many trick-or-treaters yet, but I bet you'll be my favorite this evening."

"Thanks," Peter said.

"Maya," Travis muttered.

"Yes?"

"I forgot a bag. And I forgot to leave a mouth hole in the costume, so I can't eat, dang it. Would you keep my candy for me?"

"Sure." She tucked an extra Milky Way into her messenger bag.

Wonder Woman put her basket down on a nearby table and called, "Helen! Your other friends are here!"

"Oh, good." Helen appeared behind her mother in the

hallway. She was wearing a robot costume: a big silver rectangular box for the body, with blinking colored lights and gauges on it, and a domed head with lighted eyes and a grill for a mouth. Her arms and legs were inside crinkled silver bendy tubes, and she wore silver shoes and gloves. "Hi." She waved a silver hand.

"Cool costume," Maya said.

"Wow. Yours, too. We're like silver spray-paint sisters. Hey, you guys! Glad you could make it! Want some cider? Who's the Christmas tree?"

"Travis," Maya said.

"Who's the fox?"

"My little brother, Peter."

"Hi, Peter. Rowan? Rowan? Wow, I never expected to see you here! Hi, Gwenda and Benjamin! You guys look great!"

"Thanks," said Benjamin. "You look excellent, Helen."

"*Muchas gracias.* Check out the others."

They followed the robot into a living room with red shag carpet, comfortable-looking couches, an entertainment center, and three people.

"Janine's the ninja. Tovah's the cat. Sibyl's the ghost," said Helen. She introduced Peter and Travis around, because Peter was new and Travis was unrecognizable.

Janine's black ninja pajamas and full head mask with a slot for her eyes were kind of spoiled by her winter coat, which was pink. Tovah was wearing a fuzzy white coat that blended in with her white fake-fur pants and white hat with tall pink cat ears attached. She had a white cat mask that covered her eyes and nose and sported whiskers.

Sibyl had gone the white sheet route, only her sheet was white with little blue roses all over it. It was belted at the waist with the gold scarf of Yiliss, and she wore her glasses over the eye holes. There was too much sheet for her height. She had bunched some of the sheet up and tossed it over her left arm.

"Happy Halloween," Maya said, feeling suddenly awkward. She didn't know Tovah or Janine at all, and what was she going to do about Sibyl? Did Travis know Sibyl had a *sissimi*?

"Hey, all," said the Tovah, the cat. "Let's go get candy."

They all fled the house and ran out into the night.

# TWENTY-SEVEN

The air was cool and smelled like metal. Street lights cast an orange glow on patches of sidewalk, and some houses were dark silhouettes with lighted windows. Some were entirely dark. Those with porch lights or front lights on were the ones to visit, especially if they had Halloween decorations.

Helen led the way, giving tour guide information about her neighbors. "These guys give the kind of taffy that gets your fillings if you're not careful. I think they pull it themselves. Mom makes me show her all the homemade stuff when I get home, and usually she throws it out, so it's not even worth going there—oh, you want to try it? Go on up and come back and tell us what you got."

Peter went to the door by himself. The woman who opened it cooed over his costume and gave him a plastic bag with broken bits of something in it.

"What'd I tell you?" Helen said when he came back. They moved on. "These guys usually give fruit leather. Mom makes me save it for school lunches. Hey, Gwenda, you guys are always eating special food. Will you be able to eat any of this stuff?"

"Probably Benjamin's mom will look it over and tell us what's okay for us to eat. Mostly we came because Maya invited us. I've always wondered what this was about. I've only seen it from windows. Looked fun, but strange."

Helen laughed.

Sibyl drifted back to walk with Maya; there was only room on the sidewalk for two people abreast, and the pairs kept shifting as they moved from one house to the next. "Last time I did this, I was seven years old," Sibyl muttered. "I was dressed like a ballerina, and my dad took me around. I thought it was the best holiday ever."

"Still is," Maya said.

"But Daddy—" The sheet ghost aimed her glasses toward the clump of kids ahead of them. "Daddy."

"Did the Thrixa people snatch you from your home?" asked Maya.

"No. No. Mommy and Daddy—they died. I'm pretty sure. I mean, someone else picked me up from school, someone I never met before, and she said I couldn't go home ever again, and then I went to a shelter with a lot of other kids. I was there a couple months, I think. I didn't really know how to count days yet. I was playing in the yard by the back fence when Gaelli came to talk to me. He asked me if I wanted to go somewhere else, where there were people who'd love me, and I said yes. Yes. So I did."

They visited a house, trailing behind all the others. The woman seemed pleased to see them and gave them handfuls of hard candy. Maya said, as they hit the sidewalk, "Bikos was an orphan, too."

"We all were. The Thrixa only wanted kids who didn't have family and needed a better place to go. Hey, Maya," Sibyl said.

"Yes?"

"Those kids from Janus House. Yiliss says there's something weird about them."

"Like what?"

"They're—" Sibyl jumped as Rowan strode up beside them. He was walking in the street. He glared at both of them, then moved on ahead. He hadn't brought anything to carry candy in, and he didn't go up to front doors. Mostly he just seemed to want to hang around and glare at people. Maya was surprised he'd actually gotten a scythe. He could have done all the glaring without it.

Sibyl grabbed Maya's arm and pulled her to a stop, letting the others move on. "Those Janus House kids have extra layers of energy, Yiliss says. Does Rimi know about this? Yiliss thinks there's no way she could not know."

Maya didn't know what to say.

"I mean, I've been staying away from them at school, because Yiliss and I are trying to blend in, and everybody else keeps away from them. Except you and Travis. You know, don't you?"

"I guess," Maya said.

*Evren's nearby*, Rimi said. *Just behind us. Too close.*

"What does it mean?" Sibyl asked. "What are these extra layers? What kind of different are those kids?"

"What does Yiliss think?"

"Yiliss thinks—who's there?" Sibyl turned toward Evren. Yiliss lifted fringed ends, wavered the fringes, and then all of them straightened, pointing toward nothing. "Someone's right here! Yiliss says! And I can't—Maya—"

Maya pulled out her flashlight and shone it behind

them, the direction Yiliss was pointing. Nothing was visible except empty sidewalk, fence, and rhododendron bushes. Rimi dropped shadow over Maya's eyes, enough to show her Evren's outline.

"Someone's there," Maya agreed.

"Is it a ghost?" Sibyl whispered. "You've lived on Earth all your life. Have you seen ghosts before? Or felt them? Is this what that's like?"

"I don't know. I've never seen a ghost, and I've only had *sissimi* help to see things for a few weeks," whispered Maya. "Without Rimi, I don't think I would've known anything was there." She felt suddenly overwhelmed. She didn't know how she was going to keep secrets from everyone when people kept suspecting things. Maya hated lying. For one thing, it was a strain remembering the fake stuff you made up. For another thing, it made her feel rotten. Now she was lying to her parents and her sister, and hiding things from her friends. She couldn't keep track of who knew what. When anyone asked her a direct question, she just wanted to answer. And since Rimi had lifted Harper's silence from Maya's tongue, Maya *could* answer, even when she shouldn't.

"Hey, you," she said in Evren's direction. "We know you're following us. What do you want?"

*Agitation,* Rimi thought. *And now, he's running away.*

"Yiliss said he ran away," Sibyl said. She pressed her hands against her chest. Her breathing was hard and fast. "I thought I understood Earth. Now I just don't know."

"Hey, dudettes," said a nearby Christmas tree, "you okay? You totally disappeared on us."

Maya swung the light to illuminate Travis, then aimed it at the ground. There was enough reflected light to show her Sibyl's pale, ghostly, expressionless form beside her. Maya looked at Sibyl, and Sibyl stared back, or at least her glasses and eyeholes were aimed in Maya's direction.

"Sorry," Maya told Travis. "We just wanted to talk."

"Well, come on. We're, like, a whole block ahead of you. You're missing all the fun." Travis held out a fistful of candy bars. Maya opened the messenger bag, and he dropped them in, then waved Maya and Sibyl past him. Up the street, Maya saw a shadowy group of figures. Was it the right group? Had she lost Peter, after promising her parents she wouldn't get separated from him?

The owl on her helmet hooted. *He's there, with the others. We haven't lost anybody, Mayamela. I'm keeping track of him.* Rimi sent Maya warmth. *I can remember who knows what, too. Travis doesn't know about Sibyl yet. We should tell him, maybe tomorrow, if he doesn't find out tonight.*

*Rimi*, Maya thought. *Thank you.* She gripped Sibyl's hand. "Come on," she said. "Let's stay with the others. Thanks for coming back for us, Travis." Maya pulled Sibyl back to the group.

They all approached a well-lit house with four pumpkins on the porch, different thicknesses of pumpkin rind making some of the pumpkins brilliant orange, and others shadowy globes lit from the mouth, nose, eye, and eyebrow holes. The candlelight flickered, and the air smelled of melting wax and singeing pumpkin.

Helen rang the bell. A teen boy answered the door. "Trick-or-treat," everyone yelled.

"Jeez," he said, "how many of you are there?"

"A bunch," said Helen cheerfully.

"I don't know if we have enough stuff for everybody," he said.

From deeper in the house, a woman's voice floated out. "Jerry, of course we do. Hand out the candy. We have more bags in the living room. You don't get to save it all for yourself!"

He tossed a snarl over his shoulder, but he gave candy to everybody.

Back on the sidewalk, Benjamin walked beside Maya. "This is such a weird custom," he muttered as they trailed the others toward the next house, a big old Victorian with skull lights drooping along the porch roof and a flagstone path from the sidewalk to the porch steps.

"But fun, no?" Maya asked.

He smiled wide at her. "In a lot of different ways."

*Maya,* a voice called, faint and far away.

*Rimi?*

*That wasn't me,* Rimi thought.

Maya felt a spot of heat near her right hip. She touched it and felt the lump of the rough garnet trapped in her pocket. "Oh," she said. "Oh—" She stepped off the sidewalk and looked back.

Houses lined the street, some dark, some with windows glowing, some windows masked by curtains and some revealing their insides in snapshot glimpses. Porch lights splashed over walls and ground but left deep shadows. Street lights spread globes of orange radiance, but between them stripes of darkness lay across the pavement. People, most of them pretty short, surged along the street, dark silhouettes. All light was ringed with darkness and the stretching of shadows. The air was chill against her face and hands, and freezing against the back of her neck where Rimi was not attached.

"Maya?" Benjamin said.

"I thought I heard something." Maya stared into the dark-and-light distance.

*Maya.*

"Steph?" she whispered. She took the garnet out of her pocket and held it in her hand. It was warm, but she couldn't tell if that was because of some ghostly agency or because it had been tight against her hip.

*The walls between the universes are thinner on Halloween night*, Gwenda said in Maya's memory.

*Hey, Maya.* The voice was so soft. Did it come from the dark, or from her imagination?

Rimi thought, *There's a shadow here.*

*Show me. Please.*

Rimi dropped a layer of shadow over Maya's eyes that made the night clearer and less dark. Maya saw a wavery form about five feet from her. A little shorter than she was—the same height she had been last spring—and the shadow had hair on her shadow head that didn't match Maya's last images of chemo-bald Stephanie. Lovely dandelion fuzz hair, a tight-curled mane, like Steph used to have before she got sick.

*Hey, pal.*

Everything inside Maya froze.

"Steph," she whispered. "Are you here? Is that you?"

*It's me.*

"How'd you find me?" Tears heated Maya's eyes and spilled down her cheeks. "We left, Steph. We ran away. I didn't want to leave you, and then I didn't want to do anything but sleep and cry. They made me leave."

*I know. I'm sorry you had such a tough summer, pal. There was nothing I could do.*

"I miss you so much."

*Yes. That's how I found you. I'm mostly gone, Maya, but there's still a connection between us. Thanks for keeping me in your heart.*

"Steph! You would not b*elieve* the people I know now!"

Steph laughed. More than anything else, that warble of laughter convinced Maya she was actually talking to her dead best friend.

*I get that, pal. Boy howdy do I get that.*

"I wish you were—"

*Yeah, but I'm not,* Steph said. *And that's okay. You're going to be okay.*

Maya reached up and put her hand on the cheek of her helmet. Warm, soft. Rimi, looking like metal, feeling like flesh. Maya sighed and straightened. "Yeah," she said. "I am."

The shadow Steph radiated a feeling of smile. *So,* she said, *I'm off on my next adventure. You don't have to keep me alive, Maya. I'm there all by myself, in my own way. Think of me when you want to, but don't worry about me, okay?*

"Really?"

*Really. Now that I know you're going to be all right, I'm not going to hang around anymore. Okay?*

"Do you have to go?"

*No, but I'm ready to, and I'm going to. Bye, pal. You were the best friend ever. See ya.*

"Where?"

Stephanie laughed again. *Somewhere down the road. With these new friends of yours, you'll be going lots of places. Who knows? We might bump into each other! Love you.*

The shadow vanished, and so did the sense that Stephanie was present.

"Steph!" Maya cried. She lifted her hands and rubbed her eyes. She had to sniff a few times. Then she glanced sideways.

Benjamin had formed a triangle with his fingers and thumbs, the same way Columba had before, and he was staring through that frame toward where Stephanie had stood. He separated his hands and lowered them, then looked at her.

"Did you see her?" Maya asked. Her throat was tight, and her voice came out squeaky.

"Yeah," he said. His voice was higher than usual, too. "My first ghost."

"Did you hear her?" Maya asked, a little softer.

Benjamin shook his head. "But—amazing."

"Maya, Maya, Maya!" Peter darted toward her. "Are you all right?"

"I—oh, Peter!" She wrapped her arms around him and hugged him tight.

"You're squishing my head," he said, his voice muffled by his mask.

"Oh! Sorry!" She straightened, released him, and studied his mask. She had compressed the fox's whiskery cheek so the mask had a dent in it instead of a curve.

*Lean close to him again*, Rimi thought.

Maya took Peter in her arms again and leaned close. She felt her helmet shift somehow. "I fixed it," Rimi said aloud, very quietly, and Maya let Peter go again.

"Thanks," Peter muttered. He patted his restored cheek. "Maya. Are you okay? I heard you yell."

"It was Steph, Peter! Steph's ghost! Ben saw her, too!"

"You *did*?" Peter squeaked.

"Uh—" said Benjamin.

Maya turned and stared at him. All these secrets, jammed up inside her, and she was supposed to share them with some people and not others. This one was all her own, and she wanted Peter to know it. Was Benjamin going to pretend it hadn't happened? Something bitter twisted inside her. She had told Stephanie she was going to be okay, based in part on her belief that Benjamin was one of her new best friends.

Peter would believe her, either way. Rimi would support her. Still—

"I did," Benjamin said.

Maya started breathing again. She held out her hand, and he grasped it. His hand was warm and dry, and his grip was firm, but not too tight. He pressed his thumb into her palm and then let go.

"Wow. Oh, wow. Oh wow!" Peter yelled, jumping, and then the rest of their friends returned, laughing and lugging loot.

"What's the fuss? What's going on?" asked Helen.

"Maya saw a ghost!" Peter said.

A flood of questions poured out of her friends. "Was it scary?" "Was it someone you knew?" "What did it do?" "Is it still here?"

Gwenda stopped beside Maya and waved her wand. Its crystal tip lit up, trailing sparks. Gwenda's eyes shone with reflected flickers. "Maya!" she said. "Was it Steph?"

"Yes," Maya said.

Gwenda hugged her, scattering more sparks.

"Too weird," said Travis. "Or—maybe not."

"Yil—my—I saw it, too," Sibyl said.

"You did?" said Maya.

"Kind of sensed it. A glowing outline right near you. Yil—a kind of person." Sibyl's hands were shaking. Her loot bag rustled with her shudders. "Were you scared?"

*Had* she been scared? All the feelings she'd had lately— apprehension, wonder, frustration, sorrow, the overwhelming sensation of too many secrets hanging over her head and not knowing how to organize them. Sarutha saying goodbye. Columba and Evren saying hello. Harper frowning at her, as he always did. Weyland saying she had another safe place to come. Benjamin and Gwenda coming out of the shell of Janus House and stepping into the rest of the world, where Maya and Travis lived.

Here she was, out in the Halloween-haunted night, with friends in disguise, and one friend who had unmasked by becoming a mask. She had a growing candy stash at her right hip and Rimi wrapped around her, and Steph had come back. Steph had come back. Steph knew about the magic, and she had left Maya in the heart of it, with her blessings.

"Happy," said Maya. "But Steph just came to say good-bye, and now she's gone."

"Still," said Peter. "Best Halloween ever!"

Over the past twenty-some years, **NINA KIRIKI HOFFMAN** has published novels, juvenile and media tie-in books, short story collections, and more than two hundred fifty short stories. Her works have been finalists for the World Fantasy, Mythopoeic, Theodore Sturgeon, Philip K. Dick, and Endeavour awards. Her first novel, *The Thread That Binds the Bones,* won a Bram Stoker Award, and her short story "Trophy Wives" won a Nebula Award.

Nina does production work for *The Magazine of Fantasy & Science Fiction,* and teaches short story writing through her local community college. She also works with teen writers. She lives in Eugene, Oregon, with several cats, a mannequin, and many strange toys.

To learn more about her work, visit www.ofearna.us/books/hoffman.html.